Foreword

David (of blessed memory) and I wrote this book about 20 years ago. We did not seriously explore publishing it, though some inquiries were made. And so, this book, in which my husband and I took such pleasure writing, sat patiently waiting to be read.

David passed away on April 15, 2020 of Covid19. I decided to self-publish this book as a tribute to David and because I believe this story is timely and worth telling.

The Endless Forest is a fantasy-adventure for all ages. Children are the main characters because of the association of childhood with innocence and the potential for growth. Animals are used in this story to convey qualities that we value. It is a story about life's challenges, empowerment, and transformation; it is a tale about reaching deeply into the core of the knowing self and drawing from its strength. The beauty of stories is their power to resonate at a deep and individual level; so, I hope, each reader will take something unique and personal from this tale.

The Endless Forest tells the story of 10-year-old Niles who is troubled by Calamidrake, a dragon in his head who belittles him and urges him to get in trouble. Niles attempts to appease the dragon (misbehaving to shut the dragon up in order to stop the pain of being belittled), but heeding to the dragon only makes things worse. Niles learns from his best friend Roger that Roger has also experienced the dragon. Roger tells Niles that to stop the dragon, he must embark on a journey-alone.

In the forest, Niles is befriended by a cast of offbeat animal characters each with some lesson to impart. These characters provide Niles with a foundation from which he builds the courage to confront the dragon (metaphor for crisis) and the fortitude needed to continue and complete his journey.

As Niles progresses through a series of adventures that lead towards a climactic confrontation with Calamidrake on the Bridge of Passage, the reader becomes aware of how Niles has been empowered and transformed through his journey through the endless forest. Does Niles overcome the dragon? Can anyone ever permanently overcome a dragon? Maybe, maybe not. We learn from this tale that every crisis has life-changing potential and that often pain precedes and motivates transformation, hopefully resulting in a wiser, knowing self.

And, remember, at face value, this is a delightful children's story whose surprise ending will make you smile.

It is important to note that I purposely left out access to I Phone or other technology in this story. This tale is about a boy and his journey without technological aid {can we even imagine a world like that? Let's try}).

To David, my husband and co-author, who brought color to my forest, walked with me through darkness and light, and was my bridge over troubled waters for 48 years. May his memory be for a blessing.

Table of Contents

Chapter 1- An Ordinary??? 10-Year-Old Boy

Dark and terrible secrets can be found almost anywhere, even in peacefully sleepy small towns such as Brindell-by-the-Wood. Consider the case of Niles, a more-or-less normal mischievous 10-year-old boy. Until last wintertime's long and shivery nights, Niles lived quietly in a cottage at the edge of Brindell-by-the-Wood. But with the blasts of wintery snow came a Dragon, and that changed everything.

In fact, dragons are not rare in this part of the world, but I could hardly say that they are common. You would not expect to meet one as you walked down the town streets or strolled the shady country lanes. But if you were a 10-year-old boy, or even an 8-year-old or 12-year-old boy, chances are you would have confronted at least one.

As if dragons were not enough, Brindell-by-the-Wood has another ominous secret which the adults call the "Deep Woods." It is a nearly impenetrable tangle of bent trees, thorn bushes, and who-knows what else that encloses the town to the north and east. The children know it just a little better, however, and to them it is a mysterious and sinister place that they name in whispers the "Endless Forest."

Not everyone who ventures into the Endless Forest ever returns. Indeed, some children believe that the Dragons come from the heart of the forest, but as we shall see, the truth is far more curious than that. Niles, for one, definitely intends to stay well clear of the Forest especially after all he has heard about it. And Niles has heard only the tiniest fraction of all there is to hear about that shadowy place. And a very shadowy place it is, I assure you.

But I am being terribly rude, aren't I -- I haven't even introduced you to Niles. Well, since here he is now, why don't you shake his hand? (Actually, that might not be such a good idea, since Niles may not have washed since he played with the toads by the stream). If you did shake his hand, however, you would probably say that you shook the hand of a fairly ordinary almost 11-year-old boy.

That is what his best friend Roger thought two years ago, before the Dragon came, when he wrote a poem about Niles. Perhaps you would like to read it, although, to be honest, it is not a very good poem. I'm sure you will be able to do better after you meet Niles yourself. Anyway, here is what Roger wrote:

He's not too fat.
He's not too thin.
He really likes the shape he's in.

He's not too short.
He's not too tall.
Too big or little? Why, not at all!

His eyes are blue.
His eyes are green.
Well actually, they're in between.

His hair is brown,

But rather light.
He never gets it combed just right.

And so it flops
Into his eyes,
Regardless of how hard he tries.

Nowadays, Roger would be embarrassed if he knew we were reading his poem, because he is much older (nearly 11). Besides, Roger would want us to know more about Niles, like how good a friend he is, and how funny, and how they talk about things together that they don't say to anyone else. Roger would tell us that Niles' other qualities -- his honesty, sense of humor, and loyalty, to name a few -- are much more important than whether Niles' hair flops on his eyes.

All this does not seem to make Niles seem very unusual. And if you saw him at this very moment, there would be nothing to change your opinion. Today Niles is wearing jeans, which he wears most of the time, except when his mother makes him wear dress pants for special occasions. Niles does not like wearing dress pants and has never figured out what makes special occasions so special. But, back to what he is wearing today. In addition to his usual jeans, he is wearing his old brown and green striped shirt, one of his favorites, since it was a birthday present from Roger. His shoes are old sneakers and his socks -- well, it's hard to say about his socks, because they have slumped down inside his shoes.

Yes, Niles seems ordinary, very ordinary. Right? … Wrong! Perhaps he looks happy and even a trifle boring, but the truth is very different. He is not boring at all. And he has not been happy very often since the Dragon came. No, Niles is not ordinary today, and tomorrow he will be even <u>less</u> ordinary.

Have you already figured out what is about to happen? Did you guess that Niles is about to have an adventure, and that before the Moon rises this evening, he will be deep inside the Endless Forest with no idea at all of how to get out? Perhaps you did and none of what follows will be news to you, but I promise that it would surprise Niles very much, and as to what his mother and father would say about it, I should not like even to guess!

Chapter 2 - Introducing the Dragon

Before Niles begins his adventure, there are a couple more introductions.

First there's Roger. It is fair to say that without Roger, the adventures in this tale might never have happened at all. So, surely, he is worth meeting. Now, Roger and Niles are best friends. They have known each other since they were babies. Roger is about six months older than Niles, and several inches taller. In fact, Roger is the tallest <u>boy</u> in the class, but not nearly the tallest person. Mrs. Stern, his teacher, is taller, and that's okay, but so are several girls. Unfortunately, girls at this age grow tall sooner than boys, and they can be very obnoxious about it. At least, that's the way Roger and Niles see it. The girls think most of the boys are dorks.

Getting back to Roger, we find a very neat boy. In fact, he is such a neat boy that he is almost a neat "young man." His dark brown hair is always combed perfectly when he gets to school in the morning. His shirts are always clean and his shoes are polished. Roger says his mother makes him dress that way. Niles feels sorry for him.

Roger is also very smart. He never has trouble with schoolwork and often helps his friends when they get stuck with their homework. I suppose Roger could be a royal "pain in the behind," but he isn't. He's just a nice boy, and I'm not the only one who says so.

In any case, Roger likes the same things that Niles likes, and they have the best times together. That is, they have the best times together except when Niles is in trouble, which has been all too often recently. Then Niles' mother and father ground him, and that means he has to stay home -- alone.

For example, there was the time that Niles pulled up all of the flowers in Mrs. Greenstem's garden. At least, that's what nasty old Mrs. Greenstem says he did. According to Niles, that isn't completely true -- he knows he left the small patch of daises in the corner, because they reminded him of the flowers his father brought home to his mother. Besides, Mrs. Greenstem is a pain. When she saw Niles riding his bike through a puddle (so he could splash the girls as they went by), she told his mother. What a pain! Digging up her garden was the least he could do.

You and I can understand why his Mom and Dad would ask Niles: "Why in the world did you do that?" But Niles looks at it differently. "They're always asking me the same question," Niles thinks to himself. "Why did I do this? Why did I do that? Don't they know about IT?"

IT?

If you already guessed that "IT" is a dragon, you are quite right. In fact, "IT" is a most horrid beast who appears in Niles' head, creeps into his mind, and says terrible things. "IT" is very, very large -- bigger than most thoughts and only a little smaller than imagination. It changes color depending on Niles' mood, but its head is usually a dark,

dark green (almost black) with yellow and red flashing
eyes, and bright red nostrils from which it breathes fire.

Its body is covered in scales except for its underbelly,
which is absurdly smooth and white -- from sitting on it all
these long years, I suspect. It has wings, of course -- four of
them in fact. The two large ones are almost as wide as they
are long and are attached in the usual place just behind its
front legs. The smaller pair of wings join near its shoulders
and are especially useful for fanning itself when fire
breathing makes the Dragon too hot.

This Dragon's most impressive feature is its tail,
which is extraordinarily long and flexible. "IT" can curl it
up like a hose and then whip it out with a crack like
thunder. Or, it can make a fine bed of it and actually go to
sleep hidden amidst its own tail. That's quite a trick, and
most other dragons can't come close. It makes this Dragon
so proud that it often lies down in that position even when
it isn't very sleepy.

But the times "IT" is most proud is when he can put
his ugly thoughts into Niles' head. "What sort of
thoughts?" you ask. Nasty things about the people Niles
likes, about Roger, and about Niles himself. I don't like to
repeat them, but if you read the rest of this story you will
hear quite enough.

The Dragon first appeared inside Niles' head last
winter. At first, it was silent, and stayed only for a few
minutes at a time. But as winter wore on into spring, it
appeared more often, and stayed longer. But still it was
silent. Then one day, as Niles was trying to get the Dragon

out of his thoughts, it spoke to him. Now having a Dragon appear in his head was strange, and having it speak to him was worrisome, but what it said was nothing short of alarming: "Well, I'm here now, and you better get used to it."

Since then, the Dragon has appeared many times, and whenever it comes, nasty sad thoughts fill Niles' head. Sometimes Niles talks with it, like the day Niles asked its name. The Dragon laughed wickedly and said "You can call me Sir Draconis of the Ugly Thoughts." And then he laughed again.

Since the dragon wouldn't tell its real name (they never do), Niles made up one of his own. It happened like this. One day, he heard his father talking about a terrible war that had happened long ago. "It was a calamity for this country," he had said. Niles had liked the word "calamity." It seemed to fit the Dragon very well.

The next time the Dragon appeared Niles called it Calamity." To his surprise, the Dragon got very angry. "You are stupid, indeed," it had yelled at him, blowing steam out of its nostril for the very first time. "Stupid, stupid, stupid! Don't you even know the difference between males and females?" He paused for just a moment and then went on.

"I'm a male dragon, you dolt! So why do you give me a girl's name? Calamity? Bah! If I were female, maybe that wouldn't be so bad, but I'm a drake! A drake – do you get it?" Niles didn't get it.

"A drake!" the Dragon fairly screamed. "A <u>male</u> dragon. That's what a drake is – a <u>male</u> dragon."

"Oh," answered Niles. He had no idea what else to say. He didn't like the Dragon and didn't really care what it thought, but somehow making it too angry seemed a poor idea. So from that time on, he added the word "Drake" to its name, calling the Dragon "Calamity Drake" which soon got shortened to "Calamidrake." And that is the name he calls it today.

No matter what the name, no one knows how hard Niles fights the awful feelings that the Dragon dumps on him. Luckily, it doesn't visit every day. But lately it has been coming more and more often. Niles knows that <u>something</u> must be done. But what?

Chapter 3 - Everything That Goes Up Must Come Down

Let me tell you how Calamidrake crept into Niles' world one afternoon and how it helped him; helped him get into trouble, that is.

It was a little over a month ago. The day had started out gray and drizzly, but about lunchtime the sun peeked from the clouds, a warm wind blew in from the south, and all of the wetness scurried away like rabbits surprised in an open field. By the time school ended, the sky was sunny, the birds were chirping, and even the leaves on the trees were dry.

Most of Niles' classmates were excited. They were staying at school to rehearse their parts in the school play. Niles had decided not to be in the play; the Dragon told him it was stupid. (Nice going, Calamidrake).

So, Niles walked home along the path that led past Mrs. Greenstem's garden. She had planted new flowers recently (after Niles had dug the old ones up), and they were just starting to bloom. Niles glanced at the flowers; a nasty thought flitted briefly through his head, but Niles had learned _that_ lesson.

Suddenly, Niles heard Calamidrake hissing at him. He walked faster and tried to ignore it, but it was no use. "You're a welkus," whispered the Dragon. Niles didn't really know what a welkus was (which is not surprising, since it is a word used only by Dragons). But he figured it couldn't be very nice.

Niles knew that it was just the Dragon talking, but he still couldn't help feeling sad. "I'm really not much good," he thought to himself. Calamidrake had been a pale shade of blue, but as Niles started to feel badly, he began to change color. Already light orange dotted his shoulders spread towards the middle of his back.

Once the Dragon showed up, it was hard to get rid of it. "No one wants to play with you," Calamidrake whispered, breathing just a hint of steam through its left nostril. "How do you know anyone even likes you? Do you think Roger likes you? Where is Roger now, when you're all alone?" With a smug look, the Dragon, now entirely orange, curled its tail under itself and pretended to go to sleep. But it kept one eye open.

Niles decided to find Roger. Maybe that would make "Sir Draconis of the Ugly Thoughts" shut up and go away.

Do you see how Calamidrake was controlling Niles? Niles usually reacted to what the Dragon said, even though he didn't have to. If he ever figures that out, it will be a very bad day for Calamidrake. But that day has not yet come for Niles. For some people, it never comes.

On this day, Niles did listen to the Dragon. He turned off the main path and headed back towards school. He crossed a green field dotted with wildflowers and leapt over a tiny brook lined with small bushes. Rounding a small hill, Niles ran the last steps up to the schoolyard and looked in every direction. Roger was nowhere to be seen. "Welkus," repeated the Dragon.

"I knew you weren't really asleep," answered Niles.

"I never said I was," answered Calamidrake smugly, blowing a smoke ring out of his right nostril. It swirled through the air, changing color slowly from red to orange to yellow and then suddenly disappearing with a "Pop" sound. This was one of the Dragon's favorite tricks and he was exceptionally proud of it. Niles had come to know that the Dragon blew smoke rings only when it was very pleased with itself -- and that was always bad news for Niles.

Just then, Niles happened to pass the largest tree in the schoolyard. Now his troubles were really about to begin. The tree was an old oak, so wide around that it took three people holding hands to encircle it. Its bark was dark brown, with streaks of black, with here and there a small hole carved out by a passing woodpecker. Looking up, Niles saw the first powerful branches split off the main trunk. The largest was almost, but not quite, out of his reach.

He thought to himself "Will I still be a welkus if I climb to the top of that tree?"

Calamidrake was silent for just a moment, and Niles began to feel better, but then came the Dragon's mocking voice: "You'll never do it."

The thought of climbing the big tree frightened Niles a little, but it <u>was</u> exciting. Niles liked feeling excited, because that seemed to quiet Calamidrake for a little while. Sometimes it even made it turn back to light blue, which was its best color as far as Niles was concerned.

Niles looked up at the tree. It was very tall, but Niles was thinking that if he climbed all the way to the highest branch, the other children would know how fearless and cool he was. That's what Niles was thinking. Meanwhile, the Dragon was thinking: "Now I've got him!" And you and I are thinking: "He's going to try it -- oh no!" It turns out that we are all right.

Niles was a little worried. He remembered that his teacher had often told the class not to climb that tree. He knew he might get in trouble if he broke the rule. "Maybe I should just go home," he said to himself.

"I knew you wouldn't do it. I knew it. I knew it. I knew it." That was the Dragon, of course.

Niles tried to keep the Dragon out of his mind, but the bad feelings became overwhelming. He had to do it. He had to climb the tree if he was ever going to feel better. Or so he thought.

So, Niles grabbed at the first large branch and pulled himself up into the tree. Then he began to climb. At first, the climbing was easy. Large, solid branches split off the main trunk at convenient intervals, and there were more than enough handholds and footholds. As long as he climbed, Calamidrake kept quiet.

The Dragon had promised Niles that he would feel better if he climbed the tree. But Niles remembered how Roger had warned him never to do it. As Niles imagined how disappointed Roger would have been, he felt even worse than before. That was the problem with listening to the Dragon -- things usually didn't work out the way it said they would.

Niles kept climbing. The trunk had become much slimmer, and the branches that came off it were smaller still. Trying to get around one branch that didn't seem large enough to hold his weight, Niles slipped a little and scratched his hands on the rough bark. A moment later, he almost fell when a small branch broke away under his foot.

The leaves of the tree had provided shade and kept it cool during Niles' climb, but as he neared the top, sunlight broke through from time to time. The air was still and began to feel warm and sticky. A little sweat ran down Niles' forehead, and he wished for a cool breeze like the one that had washed over him when he was halfway up the tree, but none came.

Niles did not get to the very top of the tree, since that was a tiny branch that only a very small bird could sit on, but he got very close. Sitting carefully on the last branch large enough to hold his weight, Niles felt excited and proud, and Calamidrake was completely gone from his mind.

Niles strained to feel the Dragon's presence, but could only catch a faint glimpse of it down among the mists of memory. He could tell, however, that the Dragon was a very pale shade of blue. "It doesn't get any better than this," Niles thought and for once he was right. It didn't get better. It got worse.

The first thing that happened was that Niles looked down and saw the angry and frowning face of one of his teachers, Miss Knowall, looking up at him. His classmates also gathered around looking up at him and at each other with puzzled expressions; they were smart, Niles thought, much too smart to know about the dragon. Niles looked apprehensively at the children who shared his worktable at school; perhaps they were worried that Niles might not be able to complete his part of the project that was due tomorrow. Or perhaps they were worried about him.

Next, the wind started to blow. Looking off to his left, Niles was startled to see a storm cloud building in the distance, dark gray outlined against the brilliant blue sky. A small gust of wind made the tree sway just a tiny bit, but it was enough to cause Niles to tighten his grasp around the slender trunk that led to his treetop perch.

Niles already knew he was in trouble, but he thought: "at least the other kids will know how cool I am to be able to climb this tree." And it was true - Niles could climb the tree. Well, to be exact, he could climb _up_ the tree. On the other hand, Niles soon discovered that he could not climb _down_ the tree.

Now he was almost too afraid to shift his weight. Every movement caused the top of the tree to bend. It was terribly frightening. Niles finally got up the courage to try one step, down to the branch below his seat. But as soon as he put his weight on it, the branch bent and seemed about to break. Calamidrake just laughed. Oh, yes, he was back now, and Niles was alarmed to see that most of his body was a deep orange.

All of his good feelings were gone. Now Niles felt ashamed, frightened, and a little cold. The storm was building in the West and coming closer. Niles thought he heard the rumble of distant thunder. The wind began to blow in earnest, and the treetop swayed first one way and then the other.

While Niles was wondering just what he could possibly do, the worst possible thing happened. He heard a siren coming down the street towards the school. Someone had called the Fire Department to get him out of the tree. "Just like a stupid cat," Calamidrake put in.

As the fire engine came to a stop in the parking lot, lightning flashed from the angry base of the storm cloud. The wind whistled through the branches and Niles felt his grip slipping.

Calamidrake was entirely red, just like the fire engine, except for its head. It was keeping up a stream of nasty comments, but they didn't bother Niles at all. He was far too concerned with hanging on to even listen to the Dragon.

Just then Niles heard a loud crash coming from just under him. He was afraid to look down, thinking that one of the big branches of the tree must have broken off. But the sound was actually caused by the firemen's ladder, now resting solidly against the tree trunk just a few feet below where Niles sat trembling.

When Niles saw the fireman climbing the ladder, he felt an overwhelming relief. His rescuer was only 10 or 15 steps away. Suddenly, Niles was aware of the Dragon's roar. He could feel the hot breath burn his neck. And, as if the storm was working right along with the Dragon, a dreadful bolt of lightening struck the tree next to his.

Niles shut his eyes as tightly as he could. The Dragon was now a brilliant scarlet red and was laughing so hard it couldn't even breathe fire.

Then the fireman was there, gently lifting Niles off his branch and setting him on the uppermost steps of the ladder. "Ok, pal," he heard the man say, "just climb down one step at a time. I'll be right behind you."

It seemed an eternity to Niles before he finally reached the ground. His teacher was furious, and all of the kids teased him. Niles was too relieved and too tired to care very much. He would care a lot more when he dragged himself to school the next morning.

As he sat on the ground, surrounded by his classmates, Niles wondered what else could possibly go wrong. He soon found out. A tall man, dressed like the fireman who had climbed the tree but with a different hat, came over, smiled kindly and said: "Hi, buddy, I'm Fire Chief Quenchem. It looks like you're not hurt, so we won't need to take you to the hospital. Let's just go on home to your Mom and Dad."

"Oh, great!" thought Niles.

Chapter 4 - Roger Knows All, Tells All ... or Does He?

Niles' parents reacted just as Niles knew they would. "What's gotten into you?" asked his Dad. "You could have been killed!" cried his Mom.

"They don't know," thought Niles. "They have never felt a Dragon breathing down their necks." But he said nothing. It never did any good. No one understood.

He was grounded again and, with nothing else to do, Niles went up to his room and looked out the window. The storm that had nearly thrown him from the tall tree had passed. The sun was setting in the West and shining through the ragged edges of leftover clouds; its beams lapped gently against the far horizon, now beginning to darken into night. In the next yard, other children were playing ball. Down the street he could see Roger riding his new bright electric blue bike.

Niles felt sad and angry. He remembered how Calamidrake's hot breath on his neck had made it feel like his head was on fire. Sometimes people would even tell him his face was red. Sometimes the palms of his hands got very sweaty when the Dragon talked to him. Once they were so sweaty that he slipped off the jungle gym and fell on his ... well you can imagine what he fell on. That was embarrassing.

Below him, Roger had stopped his bike and was talking with Big Albert and Little Vic. They were having fun. And here he was, all alone in his room ... again. This was the sort of thing that happened when Calamidrake popped up.

And now Niles made a mistake -- he wondered where the Dragon was.

"Right here," said Calamidrake, appearing in a cloud just above Niles' head. "Oh, no," thought Niles, "here we go again. Go away Dragon. Go away. Please."

But Calamidrake would not leave him alone. Niles felt like a little hamster stuck on his wheel, running furiously, getting nowhere. Many times he had tried to run away from the Dragon, but it always caught up to him. This time Niles just gave up in despair and waited for the Dragon to invent some new way to get him in trouble. He didn't have to wait very long.

"Just look at Roger," hissed the Dragon. "You should be out there, too. It's not fair to be stuck inside on such a beautiful day. And you know what -- I just heard your parents going out into the back yard. If you do it quickly, you can sneak out the window and be out of sight before anyone notices."

Calamidrake usually succeeded when it tried to get Niles in trouble, but not this time. Niles was feeling so badly that he didn't want to do anything ... not anything at all. He just sat there on the edge of his bed, looking out his window as day was slowly drawn up into the setting Sun and night began to fall.

"I can see this is going to be a challenge," said the Dragon, mainly to himself. "But I never give up." He thought for a moment and then he yelled at the top of his voice: "NILES, WHAT IS WRONG WITH YOU?! Are you going to let them ruin your life? Are you a boy, or are you a mouse? I hope you're not a mouse, because you KNOW what I do with mice." The Dragon puffed himself up to its full size, which was quite considerable and gave Niles its sternest look.

Actually, Niles did not know what Calamidrake did with mice. But he could make a good guess and that guess would not be good! Still, Niles was torn. He knew that if he gave in to the Dragon this time he would never again have the strength to stand up to it. On the other hand, Calamidrake was right -- Niles wasn't going to let anyone ruin his life.

There was quite a struggle going on in Niles' head, and I really can't tell you how it would have turned out had not the doorbell chosen that very moment to ring.

"Bingggggggg ... Bong." That's the way the doorbell rang in Niles' house -- first a long Bing then a short Bong. A few moments later it rang again.

Niles knew his parents wouldn't hear the bell since they were in the back yard, so he heaved himself up out of bed and slowly, very slowly, with his chin almost touching his chest, walked to the front door and opened it. It's a good thing he did, because otherwise I'm afraid this story would have quite a sad ending.

But Niles did turn the knob, and he did swing the door open, and there was Roger, leaning on his bike. "Hi, Niles. I guess you can't come out and play, but would it be okay if I came in?"

"I guess so," mumbled Niles.

Roger was a good friend, and he could easily see that Niles was very sad. So he just sat down on the comfortable tan sofa in the living room, the one with the fluffy pillows, the one that had the small tear near the top of the back which Niles had made the week before. At the Dragon's urging, of course.

Roger didn't say anything; he just sat and waited. Niles stood silently for a while, his head hung down. A tear tried to escape, but squeezing his eyes shut kept it in. Finally, he began in a whisper: "I've got a big problem."

Calamidrake was still in Niles' head. It had been impatiently waiting ever since Niles answered the doorbell. Now it began to rumble and fidget; in fact, it seemed downright nervous. The Dragon was turning a shade of green that Niles had never seen before. He wondered what it could mean.

"I know," said Roger, "I know you have a problem. But it can't be so big that we can't lick it together."

"I'm not so sure" answered Niles, sinking slowly onto the other end of the sofa. He paused for a long moment and then looked up at Roger and blurted out what he had been afraid to say to anyone else: "I have a dragon in my head."

"Not Sir Draconis of the Ugly-Thoughts!" exclaimed Roger, with more than a bit of surprise in his voice.

Niles was amazed. Roger knew about the Dragon! He stared with mouth wide open. How could Roger know? Roger almost never got into trouble, at least not recently. All Niles could think of to say was "You know Calamidrake?"

"Who's Calamidrake?" asked Roger.

"He's the Dragon," answered Niles excitedly. "That's what I call him, but he said his name was Sir Draconis."

"Oh, yes, that's him," said Roger. "Remember last year? I was always getting into trouble. Then I didn't even show up at the school picnic." Niles nodded; he remembered that well enough. Everyone was really worried about where Roger could be. Little David suggested that Roger had been devoured by a hungry bear. The rest of the class had laughed at that, but maybe Little David had been closer to the truth than anyone had imagined.

As Roger continued, a tiny bubble of hope formed in Niles' brain. "Well, that was the time when the Dragon wanted to take
over my world. I was desperate. I had to figure out a way to stop him once and for all."

"What did you do?" breathed Niles, hardly daring to hope.

"I had to go on a journey."

"A journey?" asked Niles.

"Yes, a journey -- an adventure really. It's a special kind of trip, not really very much like a vacation. What you do is seek answers to questions, or questions to answers, and along the way you have to overcome many obstacles. When I completed the journey, the Dragon lost all of its power over me."

Niles sat there speechless. His heart was pounding with a hope he had not dared to believe existed. Calamidrake was roaring in his head, but he wasn't making any sense. After a moment, Niles asked: "Who do I go with?"

"Well," said Roger, "at first you may feel you are going by yourself, and at the end you realize you were never alone."

"Alone at first?" thought Niles. That sounded scary, but he didn't want to say that out loud. So he asked, "How long does this journey last?"

"As long as it takes," answered Roger.

"What does that mean?"

"You'll figure it out," answered Roger. Niles was a little confused by this answer, but he trusted Roger. Niles would have tried anything to control the Dragon, even to the point of setting out alone in search of answers to questions, or questions to answers, whatever that meant.

After several long and silent moments, Niles finally whispered a question: "Suppose I go on this journey, and then I don't finish it?"

Roger looked at him, a tight small smile on his lips, but his big brown filling with worry. He didn't say anything. There was nothing he could say, because Roger knew that down the road of journeys not completed lay madness and pain and other things too terrible to contemplate. Finally, he said: "You have to finish it."

Chapter 5 - Niles Turns Left ... And That's Right!

The days of late spring rolled swiftly by. Niles was drawn to the journey Roger had told him about, but he was also afraid. Oddly, Calamidrake left him alone most of the time. Niles couldn't know it, but the Dragon was very disturbed. The last thing he wanted was for Niles to go on this "journey."

Yet, in the end, Dragons are Dragons. What else could they be? And what they are leads them to plant ugly thoughts in people's heads. So, after a week or so, Calamidrake crept cautiously back. When that happened, Niles had ugly thoughts. Ugly thoughts led to hard feelings. Hard feelings led to bad behavior. Bad behavior led to trouble. Again!

If Calamidrake wanted to keep Niles from going on a journey, it was doing exactly the wrong things. The more the Dragon got Niles in trouble, the more Niles wanted to begin the journey.

And so it finally happened. It was a sunny Thursday, but Niles had gone through a particularly bad day at school. Calamidrake had been breathing fire down his neck. He had gotten into trouble with the teacher and was sent to Principal Wheatley's office. The plain white walls of the principal's office depressed Niles, and the lecture from Mr. Wheatley was sad and boring. Niles had heard it all before.

As soon as Principal Wheatley set him free, Niles ran out of the office and began to look for Roger. He found him at the corner, talking with a girl. Normally Niles would have teased Roger about the girl, but there was no time for that today. Niles fidgeted until the girl left, and the moment she was gone, blurted out his question: "How do I begin the journey?"

"Are you sure you're ready?" asked Roger.

"I'm as sure as I'll ever be," replied Niles.

"Okay," said Roger, "what you do is start out towards the Endless Forest, and then just go where you need to go." He said a few things about the "Right" path and going left, but Niles wasn't paying close attention. The "Endless Forest" had shaken him quite badly.

When Roger had finished talking, Niles realized that nothing made any sense. You might agree with him now, but let me assure you that that's the way journeys are, at least in the beginning. Sometimes they end that way too, and that, of course, is the real problem.

As Niles walked slowly home, he was deep in thought. Without hardly knowing it, he took out his key and opened the front door. No one was home, shadows ruled the silent living room, and the house felt ominously empty. Niles tossed his school books onto the sofa and headed directly for the garage. His backpack was sitting on the lowest of the garage shelves, bright blue and very dusty.

Niles remembered how pleased he had been when his parents gave it to him on his last birthday. Looking at it now, he thought about them and for a moment almost decided not to go after all. But only for a moment.

"What shall I pack?" thought Niles. "I'll need so many things; there's no room for all of them."

Now you might select lots of food and maybe some clothes, but Niles chose differently. Instead, he took the things he loved the best: his favorite book, a small stuffed bear, a treasured soccer card. He packed a jar of his favorite crunchy peanut butter, his favorite strawberry jelly, and a loaf of bread. A spare pair of socks, his red miniature Ferrari racing car, and he was done. Somehow, everything just managed to fit in the backpack.

I suppose Niles never thought about where he would sleep, because he didn't even look for his sleeping bag. And you can surely think of any number of other things that he should have taken but didn't. However, Niles was anxious to start, and his backpack was already very heavy.

In fact, Niles considered leaving some of his stuff behind to lighten the load. But he <u>had</u> to take along his favorite things. After all, he didn't know how long a journey should last. And when he was scared, lonely, sad, and even angry, his favorite things made him feel better. They made him feel ... well, I should like to say they made him feel "safe," but it was more than that. They connected him with the happiness of the world and made the pain of "Sir Draconis of the Ugly-Thoughts" a bit more bearable.

And, so, Niles left his home, backpack on his shoulder. With one last look behind, he stepped out onto the path that led to the Endless Forest. He had only traveled a very short way down the path, not even up to Mrs. Greenstem's garden, when he began to feel really afraid.

His hands trembled and he began to sweat, even though there was a cool breeze blowing. At first, he could not remember when he had been so scared, but then he recalled a very tall tree and children on the ground who looked like little ants, and the branches that bent and swayed every time he tried to take a step down. It felt a lot like that time.

The path turned north, away from the Sun and towards the shadows of evening that were already beginning to form on hedges and trees. A pine swayed in the wind and dropped the last of the previous year's cones right in front of him. Most times, Niles would have stepped on it to hear the cone crunch, or at least kicked it as far down the path as he could. But not today.

Niles' fear had been growing, and now it was so strong that it was about to paralyze him. Calamidrake started breathing fire down his neck and called him mean names. Niles couldn't know it, but this was the Dragon's last desperate attempt to stop Niles from going on his journey. And it might have worked had not Niles been so stubborn -- or shall we just say "determined."

Even so, the Dragon was exceptionally persuasive, shouting its worst insults and whipping its tail about excitedly. All might have been lost had Niles not put his hand into his pocket at just the crucial time. And there he felt his lucky stone, cool and smooth against his hand.

He had forgotten to pack it, along with many other things, but the lucky stone had a way of being there when Niles needed it. And it was today. Niles brought the stone out of his pocket and looked at it. To some it would have appeared totally ordinary, but Niles loved its shine and the flecks of red that glittered against its dark gray background. The stone reassured Niles. The burning on his neck felt better.

As he rubbed the stone, Niles remembered when Calamidrake had tried to convince him to throw it away. Fortunately, Niles had not listened. Instead, he kept the stone hidden in his top drawer with his soccer cards and his marbles. Now it gave him the resolve to continue on his way.

The wind blew, but not too hard; there were no storm clouds in the sky. This was fortunate, because Niles had forgotten to bring a raincoat or umbrella, along with many other things. But Niles wasn't thinking about that because he had a bigger problem. "Where do I start?" he thought. The path led to the edge of the Endless Forest, but where it went from there he didn't know.

Niles thought very hard, trying to remember what Roger had told him. "Walk along the edge of the Endless Forest," he had said, "until you find the Right Path into the Forest. Turn left onto the Right Path and your journey will begin." That sounded fine, except for one thing. Where

<u>was</u> the Right Path and how would he know it when he found it?

This could have been quite a problem; almost insurmountable you might say. But this was not Niles' day to quit. And whoever or whatever watches over boys in need steered Niles along the edge of the Forest for a short way, until a faint and almost overgrown path entered from the left. Niles knew this was "it"--the Right Path. So, he turned onto the trace, never looking back, and he entered the Endless Forest by the Right Path. He would not turn back now, at least not until his courage failed.

Niles wondered how long that would be.

Chapter 6 - When a Rat Is Not a Rat

Walking inside the Forest was not very different from walking outside of the Forest, except that there were more trees. However, Niles soon noticed that the wood had a feel of darkness to it. The Sun was still warm, but there was a soft coolness in the air at the same time. It was odd. A vague fear grew in Niles' mind. We do not like things that are strange and unusual; they make us anxious. And then we imagine all sorts of threatening things. Niles wondered what would happen if he turned around. Would the rest of the world still be where it was a moment before?

Slowly he turned his neck around to see.

It wasn't.

No matter in which direction Niles looked, everything was the same. Trees with dark bark reached towards the sky. Their leaves appeared black as they towered high above him. A few weak sunbeams penetrated through the canopy of the treetops and made their way down to the dim forest floor.

The path he was on was clear enough and seemed to go on forever both in front of him and behind. But nowhere was there a hint of anything but the Forest. Niles was no coward, but he was totally unprepared for this. It was as if the Forest had swallowed him. A growing terror began to clutch at his heart, and he felt hundreds of fluttering butterflies in his stomach. He wondered what lay ahead, and he worried about strange things that could be lurking in the darkness.

His first impulse was to turn around and run back to the safety of his home. But he remembered what his friend Roger had said. "Once you take the first step, you must keep going forward." Besides, there was no path that appeared to lead out of the Forest, so where would he run? Niles gathered all the courage he knew, and some other that he found in unexpected parts of his mind and heart. He clasped his lucky stone in his right hand and took another step forward. And then another ...

As his eyes began to adjust, Niles realized that the forest was not really dark. He became less frightened and he started breathing more evenly. He had learned a long time ago, when the Dragon was at its worst, that he could use a trick to calm himself. While he was breathing in, Niles counted to five, and then while he was breathing out, he counted to five again. Breathing this way worked for Niles with the Dragon, and it worked just as well in the Endless Forest.

As he breathed in and out, counting to five each time, Niles felt his heart slow back to its normal rate. Gradually, he unclenched his fists and stopped biting into his lip. It was fortunate that Niles had been able to calm down, because in just a short minute Niles' heart would be set a-thumping all over again.

For now, as he looked around, Niles thought he recognized familiar things like flowers and trees. But these were the oddest-looking trees, and the flowers were very strange too. Some of the trees had bark that looked like alligator skin -- rough-edged pieces like a jigsaw puzzle waiting to be completed.

The flowers, though, were soft and beautiful, swaying gently in the cool wind. They all seemed to bend almost to the ground, but Niles could not see even one broken stalk. He had never seen such flexible stems.

"Well," thought Niles, "there's a lot in this Forest that I don't understand, but so far nothing to scare me. The path is clear and wide and completely lined with soft pebbles, and ..." Niles paused.

"*Soft* pebbles?" he said to himself, since there was no one else to hear him (or so he believed). "Soft? Pebbles are not supposed to be soft ... are they?"

The pebbles fascinated Niles, so it was only a moment before it stopped bothering him that they seemed to be soft and hard at the same time. The pebbles came in all shapes and sizes. Niles had never seen so many shapes and so many sizes, and now here they were, right under his feet. Niles was not used to noticing how things felt to his touch, but here in the Forest it seemed important to use all of his senses, not just his eyes.

Then there was another strange thing -- everything in the Forest seemed dark, but Niles' eyes had adjusted and he could still see very clearly. Then suddenly, Niles figured it all out. Everything around him was black and white. There were no colors! The Endless Forest looked dark because there were no colors in it.

Amazed at what he had seen and felt, Niles continued slowly along the path as it wound gently among the dark tree trunks. As he passed a particularly large tree that stood just at the edge of his path, he was startled by a quick movement in the distance. Peering into the light and darkness, at first Niles recognized nothing. But then he saw the rat, and a very strange looking rat it was!

At first, he was a little afraid, but Niles had always liked animals. So, he took a few breaths and a few counts to five, and then bent down and parted the branches of a low-growing bush to get a better look at the rat.

"What a weird rat," he thought to himself. Niles had never seen a rat with a long, sleek, furry body. "Maybe it's not a rat," he considered, "since I don't think rats have such clever black eyes or such beautiful markings on their faces. It looks like it's wearing a mask."

Niles was terribly curious; he moved slowly and cautiously toward the weird rat. He did not want to scare the curious animal away because it reassured him not to be alone in this black and white Forest.

As he approached the sleek little creature, he spoke softly to it. "Hello, little rat," he said as he smiled. He was about to urge it not to run away, but instead he got the surprise of his life. The small animal stood on his hind legs and spoke.

Yes, it actually and truly spoke. Talked. Conversed. Right out loud. If you don't believe me, just ask Niles.

"And what did it say?" you ask skeptically. I'll tell you, and before I do, you must put aside your disbelief. This is the Endless Forest, and things in the Endless Forest are not the same as they are in the rest of the world. Talking animals are by no means the oddest things you will find here.

Where were we? Oh, yes, the small animal stood on his hind legs and spoke in a surprisingly strong and indignant voice. "I am not a rat!" he exclaimed. "I don't even look like a rat. I can't believe you could think that. Look at this long, elegant, sleek body. Does this look like an ugly rat?"

The animal lifted itself up on its hind legs and folded its front legs over its furry chest. Standing this way, it was not quite one foot tall. Niles stood with his mouth open and stared. When the silence was finally broken, who should we hear from but Calamidrake, sleeping all this time, but now suddenly very awake. Rearing its ugly head, it snarled at Niles: "You are *really* stupid!" it said.

Niles started feeling stupid, but only for the shortest of moments. Because just then the sleek rat-like creature began yelling: "This is none of your business, you ugly twisted Dragon. Anyone can make a mistake. Go away. Breathe your ugly hot air somewhere else." The little creature had used his most authoritative tone, and the Dragon promptly shut up, curled itself around its tail and tried to look very small.

Niles' jaw dropped open in shock. "You can see it?" he stammered. "You know it's there?"

"Oh, sure," said the little animal. "We get lots of visitors down this path. Many bring along the Dragon. It's always hotter when he's around. No, no, no, Sir Draconis, as it likes to call itself, is a visitor to this Forest, but not a welcome one."

Niles was delighted. "You mean he's gone for good - - at least as long as I'm in the Forest?"

The animal gave him a questioning look. "That's up to you," it said as it dropped backed down to its normal stance, with all four paws firmly on the ground.

Chapter 7 - "Frederick Ferret at Your Service"

Niles tried to put everything that had just happened together in his mind, but it was hard. He felt a strong need to sit down on the carpet of grasses and soft pebbles. And so, he did. "Who are you?" he asked, "Or what are you?"

"Frederick Ferret, at your service," responded the small but most awesome creature. "I live in this forest, except when I don't."

"A ferret?" responded Niles, mostly to himself. "A ferret in the Endless Forest?" He paused for a moment staring at Frederick to convince himself that what he saw and what he heard were real. Niles half expected to wake up from a dream and find the ferret gone, but with each passing moment he became more convinced that this was actually happening.

"Wait until I tell Roger about you!" exclaimed Niles, coming abruptly to his senses. He was getting excited how. "Will you stay with me on this journey? Can I call you Freddie?"

"Freddie?" the ferret replied with obvious distaste. "Why on Earth would you want to call me that? 'Frederick' is so much nicer. Yes, yes, yes. 'Frederick', that's my name." He slid over and sat next to Niles on the forest floor, raising his head to peer into the boy's eyes. "Don't worry," he went on, "I will be with you. As long as you need me." Giving him a shifty sideways glance, Frederick added, "at least as long as you call me Frederick."

And so, Niles met his first friend in the Endless Forest. It would not be his last, not by a long shot. And that's also how Niles handled his first big surprise in the Endless Forest. That, too, would not be his last.

After a few minutes of rest, Niles got back up and resumed his journey. Frederick was an excellent traveling companion. Niles felt very lucky to have found him. Hmm, he had not even been looking-how lucky is that?! Whenever Niles wanted to talk, Frederick was there, full of interesting information and always ready to listen to whatever Niles had to say. They talked about the Forest, about the world outside, about Niles' friends (especially Roger, whom it turned out Frederick already knew somehow). Finally, Niles got up the courage to ask about Calamidrake.

Frederick seemed to know all about the Dragon, although he didn't call him Calamidrake. That was hardly surprising, since Niles had made up that name. Frederick didn't say much about it, however, not even when Niles asked direct questions. "That Dragon has no place here," muttered Frederick once, and after that he was silent. Yet Niles had seen the ferret tell Calamidrake to go away, and the Dragon had gone. Niles wondered if he could do the same thing. "Maybe I'll try it when the Dragon comes back," he thought.

And they walked together and talked together, continuing on the Right Path, heading deeper and deeper into the endless black and white forest. Having Frederick at his side comforted Niles. He was the cutest, cuddliest little creature he had ever seen, with lovely black and white markings, although mostly he was various shades of brown and tan. In this black and white world, Niles especially enjoyed the shades of brown and tan.

With Frederick scurrying along next to him, Niles began to feel his senses come alive. He began to smell and to enjoy the different scents of the flowers. He thought he could smell honeysuckle, orange blossoms, gardenia, and jasmine, his favorite backyard flowers.

He liked the honeysuckle best of all; he could remember the beautiful yellow honeysuckle flowers that grew in the woods near his home. Sometimes he had gone to pick them and smell the sweetness. They had calmed him somewhat when Calamidrake had been particularly nasty. Now, in the midst of the Endless Forest, the same smell brought a flood of memories and gave Niles the desire and the courage to go on.

Frederick noticed that Niles was daydreaming. "What are you thinking?" he asked. "I'm just smelling the honeysuckle," answered Niles, "and remembering the beautiful yellow flowers."

"Yellow?" questioned the ferret. "No, no, no. Not yellow. Not in this part of the forest anyway. Here the honeysuckle flowers are white, pure white. Not yellow, not yet."

Niles wondered what Frederick meant by "not yet."
But yellow or white, it didn't seem to matter. Especially
since he had begun to notice the feel of the ground beneath
him, both soft and hard at the same time. His sense of touch
was sharper here in the forest than he could ever remember
it. He felt the different shapes of the pebbles as he stepped
on them. Some were spring-like and seemed to almost
bounce him along; others were slippery and made him feel
like he was on his skateboard.

Each step brought Niles a new experience -- some
exciting, some funny, and others surprising. He could feel
the strength of the Earth beneath him. At times Niles
seemed to float, but at the same time, the ground was
always firmly under his feet.

As Niles became familiar with the forest and used to
its ways, the meandering path became easier and easier for
him to follow. Niles enjoyed having Frederick with him,
although the ferret had developed a habit of disappearing
and then popping up again a minute or two later. Niles
didn't know where Frederick went to on these little
excursions, but once the ferret reappeared chewing on
something. Niles wasn't sure he wanted to know what it
was.

Niles walked slowly along, half awake and half in a
daydream, and probably would have kept on that way for I
don't know how long, but the Endless Forest is an ever-
changing place. You must grow along with it, like the
bushes and trees, or you abandon your journey and leave
the forest entirely. Those are usually the choices the
Endless Forest gives its travelers.

And so, Niles was startled awake by a deep booming sound. He couldn't tell the direction from which the sound came, and when he turned to ask Frederick, the ferret had disappeared again. "Boom! Boom!" the sounds came again, in quick succession, and now the ground began to shake. He heard the crash of tree branches as something -- obviously something very large -- broke through the forest. Niles thought that the sounds were to his right and slightly ahead of him, although he couldn't be sure. Whatever their direction, they were definitely coming nearer! It was very ominous. Niles didn't know what kind of dangers lurked in the Endless Forest, but this sounded very much like one of them.

There was a particularly violent crash and Niles thought he could hear chanting, or maybe it was just shouting. It sounded like "Moozeslooz, Moozeslooz," but it was in a very deep voice and seemed to be quite excited or maybe angry.

Frantically, Niles looked around for Frederick. When he couldn't find him, he sought the shelter of a large tree. It was far too smooth to climb, so all Niles could do was hide behind it and hope for the best. Niles remembered all of the terrible stories people told of the Endless Forest, and he wished he had never begun this journey.

Just when Niles' fears had almost overcome him, a huge dark shadow passed by and stopped on the path not fifteen feet from the tree where Niles was hiding. The sounds of snorting and stamping on the ground were all around. The bushes were shaking and small nuts that looked a little like acorns fell from a nearby tree. Gathering what courage he had left, Niles peered around the corner of the tree. And then ...

And then he laughed and stepped out onto the path. It was a moose. Now a moose can be dangerous, especially one as large as this moose. But Niles had been so frightened, and had imagined such horrifying possibilities, that when it all turned out to be "just" a moose, he was terribly relieved. He even smiled, since as I said before, Niles really liked animals.

The moose was blinking his eyes and looking around, but it hadn't seen Niles yet. It kept singing to himself "the moose ... is loose, the moose ... is loose," which of course is what Niles had heard just moments before.

As it shook its head a few times, Niles noticed that the moose had beautiful antlers, which gleamed like dark velvet. It turned towards Niles and saw him for the first time. Niles noticed the deep soulful eyes and thought that they seemed almost sad. But the moose was obviously very, very happy, smiling and lifting its feet in a very excited way.

He was about to try to talk to the moose when Frederick reappeared, sticking his head around its front leg. "I see you have already met Hugh," he said, to which Niles could only nod in agreement. "He's really quite a nice fellow. You can come nearer. He won't hurt you." Frederick might have gone on and on, as he was wont to do, but the moose, prancing around in excitement, at that very moment stepped on the tip of the ferret's swishing tail.

"Ouch!" Frederick protested. "Be careful!"

"Sorry," replied the moose in a deep booming voice, but he kept on moving about with quick little fidgety steps. Frederick decided it would be prudent to get out of the way, and so he came over to where Niles was standing in the road. This was a safe distance from the over-stimulated moose.

"Where did he come from?" Niles asked his friend.

"Old Hugh?" answered Frederick. "Why, he's a comic strip moose you know. Yes, yes, yes. He's the famous 'Hugh Mongus.' In the newspaper comic section every day. And on television Sunday mornings. But he's gotten loose." "Loose?" questioned Niles. "Loose from what?"

"Loose from the comic strip, of course. Every so often he breaks out of the comic strip. Then he comes charging directly into the Endless Forest. He's looking for Lost Lake, you know." At the mention of Lost Lake, Hugh picked up his head and looked inquiringly at Frederick, but Frederick just shook his head sadly.

"No, I didn't know," said Niles, "but why would he want to find a lake? And besides, I haven't seen any water at all in the forest, and certainly not a lake."

Frederick gave Niles an exasperated look. "Do you think you've seen everything there is to see in the Endless Forest? You haven't seen even one thousandth of it.

There's lots of water in the Forest. Like the Slow River. Just a little further along. And many lakes."

"Okay, okay", laughed Niles, putting up his hands as if to ward off an attack. "But have you ever seen Lost Lake?"

"No," replied the ferret, "but it's here somewhere."

"How do you know?" Niles continued, moving slightly closer to the moose, who was now chomping on the soft and delicious looking foliage of the leafy plants that grew all along the path.

Frederick looked intently at Niles and said slowly, "I know Lost Lake exists, because the Moose needs it. If you need something, it can always be found in the Endless Forest."

"Why does he need the Lost Lake?"

"You do have a lot of questions, don't you," replied Frederick, but he wasn't really angry. "If Hugh can find the Lost Lake, then he will become a real moose. If *they* find him first, he will go back to being a paper animal. He's been trying for years."

Niles' face grew long with concern. "Will he ever find Lost Lake?" he asked. He wondered how anything as alive as Hugh could be bound onto a piece of paper.

"If he keeps trying, he will find something," Frederick reassured him. "It may not be what he thought he was looking for. But it will be what he was meant to find. In the Endless Forest, the only thing you must do is to keep trying."

Suddenly, Frederick turned his head and became very alert. "They're coming for him," he said.

Niles heard voices and the sound of branches being pushed aside. He could almost make out what the voices were saying. Hugh heard them too and bolted off the path and into the Endless Forest. In a moment he was out of sight, but he made a terrible racket as he crashed through the bushes and young trees.

The men's voices were nearer now. "He came this way," Niles could here one of them say. And another replied, "Yes, he certainly leaves an easy trail to follow. We should have him in a few minutes. Silly moose. Well, this time we'll find him before he hurts himself."

Niles hid behind a tree again, but Frederick stayed where he was, out in the open. "Come over here and hide," Niles whispered urgently, but the ferret didn't move and replied in a normal voice, "It's not necessary. They aren't part of your story or mine. No, no, no. They won't bother us."

And, indeed, at that moment several man-shaped shadows appeared out of the trees, crossed the path, and disappeared into the forest on its far side, heading in the direction that Hugh had taken. Niles thought that one of them glanced briefly in his direction, but he couldn't be sure. Frederick stared into the forest where the shadows had gone and sighed.

"We should've helped Hugh," declared Niles, brushing off some leaves that had stuck to his shirt. "Those terrible men will catch him now for sure. He makes so much noise!"

"You couldn't have affected the shadows," answered the ferret, still peering through the enclosing trees. He turned to face Niles, slowly walked over to him, sat down and began scratching himself with his hind paws (ferrets dearly love to scratch). "I told you, they are not part of our stories. In this Forest, we cannot affect the shadows. And they can do nothing to us. Sometimes we can see them if the Forest wants us to. That's all. You must make your own journey. Hugh must make his."

"And you're wrong about the men -- they're not bad. They aren't trying to hurt Hugh. They think they're helping him. No, no, no, they are not evil men. They just don't know how to take another's perspective, seeing only their own."

And that was all Frederick would say, although Niles, as always, would have been happy to ask questions until there were no questions left to ask -- which of course would never happen! So, Niles just got up, dusted himself off, picked up his backpack, slung it over his shoulder, and set off again down the Right Path through the Endless Forest towards ... well, towards wherever he was going, he supposed.

Chapter 8 - Sandwiches By A River

Black and white, black and white all the time -- it made Niles uneasy. There should be more color! The only real colors Niles had seen so far were the brown and tan in Frederick's coat. Maybe nothing was wrong, but certainly something was not entirely right.

One thing that Niles had just noticed was that there were different *shades* of white and black. The sunlight filtering through the black tree tops made some of their leaves look almost like dark purple and others dark blue. A few of the white honeysuckle flowers had by chance captured a sunbeam and shone brilliantly, while their shaded neighbors were a deeper and more subdued white.

It was an exciting discovery, in its way, and Niles wanted to share it with Frederick, but once again the ferret was gone. This wasn't the first time his friend had disappeared. Up until now, he had always eventually returned. But this time Niles began to worry.

Besides, the forest was noiseless and unnaturally still. As dim formless fears began to awaken in the corners of Niles' mind, finding Frederick became more and more urgent. Niles stared wildly first in one direction and then another, trying to penetrate the deep forest for any sign of the ferret. But the shadows of the trees were deep and the Endless Forest gave no sign.

A world with no sound at all can be very fearsome if you are not used to it. As the uncanny and loud silence persisted, Niles became desperate to hear something — anything. He shut his eyes as tightly as he could and concentrated. At first there was nothing, but gradually, and to his great relief, Niles began to hear something, faint and far away.

It was the wind blowing gently against the trees and flowers, each of which made its own distinctive tone. Niles had been to a concert once, and he could now imagine the honeysuckle making sounds like the flutes he had enjoycd so much. The big leafy trees sounded like cellos, and the jasmine like gentle violins.

As Niles relied less on his sight and more on his other senses, he began to hear, feel, and smell more things. Some were familiar and reassuring; some were mysterious. There was a tinkling sound that reminded Niles of rain drops. He looked up at the clear grey sky, but there were no clouds to be seen.

And there was another faint sound off to his left, coming from somewhere deeper in the forest. Niles heard it for a few moments and then it stopped, only to start up again from a slightly different place.

Niles remembered the stories about poisonous snakes in the Endless Forest and he began to worry. But there was something about the sound that he recognized. It didn't sound like any snake he had ever heard before. Niles listened harder and closed his eyes as tightly as he could.

The sound came more frequently now and was a little louder. He knew he should be careful but Niles was determined to explore this forest and to learn from it. He couldn't do that if he always ran away or hid. That is why Niles stayed where he was and tried to figure out what could be making the sound.

At the moment, Niles didn't call what he was doing anything, but you or I would probably call it "courage". Niles had always been daring. He often did risky things. But that is a long way from true courage. Yet Niles had the real thing within him and now it was coming out, prodded by the Endless Forest and helped along by curiosity.

With a louder "thump," the noises stopped. In the silence that followed, Niles realized that the last thump had been directly behind him. He was almost too afraid to open his eyes. Slowly he turned around and let his right eye open just a slit.

This time Niles was lucky. The sound could have been made by something truly dangerous, and, if it were, I hate to think
about what could have happened to him. But it wasn't, and as Niles opened his eye just enough to see what had made the sound, he looked directly into the amused face of a ferret peering inquisitively up at him.

"Freddie!" he exclaimed happily, "am I glad to see you!"

"If you mean Frederick," came the reply, "I am happy to see you too. You look worried. I hope you're not still anxious. Because of that moose, I mean."

"No, no." said Niles, "I'm fine."

He could have explained about closing his eyes and hearing the noises, but he really didn't want to. Mostly, it had been a fine experience and he wanted to keep the good parts in his mind. Besides, now he could "hear" Frederick, since he knew the sounds he made, and that was very comforting.

"Oh, sure, you're just fine. You were so scared I thought you were going to dig your head into the ground like an emu." Calamidrake was back! So much for the warm feelings that seeing his new friend had brought to Niles.

"You mean an ostrich," replied Niles. "Ostriches hide their heads in the ground, not emus. And my teacher tells me that even that isn't true -- they don't really."

Suddenly Niles remembered the trick that Frederick had used to get rid of the Dragon. This would be a good time to try it.

"Now go away," he continued in the sternest voice he could muster. But he didn't sound like the ferret. His voice was unsure and it trembled a little. "And don't come back," he added, but not convincingly.

At first Calamidrake turned away, but as Niles went on, and his tone became less and less assured, the Dragon turned back, and finally started laughing. "Emu, ostrich, who cares?" he snarled. "And if you think you can get rid of me that easily, it shows how dumb you really are." The Dragon's neck was turning red and steam trickled out of his left nostril. Soon, Niles knew, his own neck would begin to feel hot.

Niles looked hopelessly at Frederick, watching silently but with a concerned expression. He wanted to tell the ferret what had happened, to ask for help, but somehow, he couldn't. Fortunately, he didn't have to. Frederick knew exactly what was going on.

"No, no, no," said Frederick. "That's not how. "Let the Dragon know that _you_ are in charge. Not him. It is your mind, after all. You can do whatever you want with it."

That made sense to Niles, and he saw doubt in the Dragon's eyes while Frederick was talking. "He's right, Calamidrake," Niles announced in a firm voice. "It _is_ my mind, and I want you to leave. Now!"

And the Dragon did.

"Wow!" was the only thing that Niles could say. He looked at Frederick, expecting his friend to be just as surprised as he was, but the ferret just said "You wouldn't have something to eat, would you?" I've found some small nuts and a few berries. There's not much for ferrets to eat in this part of the Endless Forest." Frederick eyed Niles' backpack and sniffed in its direction.

The backpack was still on his back, and it was beginning to feel quite heavy. Niles had thought of leaving some of his things behind to lighten the load, but everything he brought was necessary. They made him feel safe, and feeling safe was important to Niles. He was not ready to leave them behind, even though he was beginning to feel safer in the Endless Forest.

"I do have some food in here," Niles told his friend. "Do you want to stop and have a meal?"

"Not quite here," answered Frederick, "There's a nicer place. Just a few minutes down the path."

Niles was getting hungry too but the "nicer place" sounded interesting. He shouldered his backpack, and he and Frederick strode rapidly forward away from the setting Sun. Shortly the travelers came to the banks of a river. A few bushes, an occasional tree, and here and there a patch of tall marsh grass separated them from the rich, black, and almost motionless water.

They came to a small clearing where two trees had fallen just to the side of the path. They made convenient seats, and several of their branches folded over one another so that, for all the world, they looked like a picnic table. "This is the place," Frederick announced.

Happily, Niles stopped, shrugged off his backpack and put it down on one of the trees. He sat down beside it and opened the clasps to the largest compartment. "You do eat peanut butter and jelly sandwiches, don't you?" he asked his friend.

"But of course," said Frederick, "as long as you have strawberry jelly and chunky peanut butter." Which is *exactly* what Niles did have!

"What luck," thought Niles, taking out his loaf of bread, the chunky peanut butter, and the strawberry jelly. He cut two generous slices of bread with his camping pocket knife, and then used it to spread peanut butter on them.

Frederick watched him curiously. "Why did you spread peanut butter on the bread?" he asked.

That seemed like a curious question to Niles, but he answered: "To hold the jelly in when I put it on top of the peanut butter. Otherwise, the jelly seeps through the bread and gets messy."

Frederick did not seem convinced. "When you make my sandwich, would you please spread jelly on the two pieces of bread, and then put the peanut butter in between?" he asked. "I *like* strawberry jelly seeping through my bread."

"Odd little creature," thought Niles.

But he was beginning to learn that just because someone did things differently than he did, that didn't mean their way was wrong. It was just different.

Niles and his ferret friend enjoyed their dinner under the growing shadows of friendly trees and beside the calm waters of the river. Frederick's sandwich had jelly seeping through the bread, and Niles' did not. But both travelers were happy with their meal.

Eating peanut butter and jelly sandwiches can make you thirsty, and Niles had nothing to drink since entering the Endless Forest. He thought about the river, but he wasn't sure it was safe to drink from it. The river looked so dark and forbidding.

That didn't bother Frederick, however. Hopping down from his tree seat and shaking a few crumbs out of his coat, the ferret scampered over to the riverbank. Then he paused and seemed to say something to the water, but Niles couldn't make out what it was. When he was finished, Frederick bent down and drank deeply. Then he splashed water from his paws onto his face and settled down next to a small tree.

That was good enough for Niles. He kneeled down next to the river, bent over and cupped his hands. As he began to dip them into the water, Frederick interrupted. "Better ask first," he warned.

"Ask what? Ask who?" questioned Niles, confused.

"Ask the river if it's okay to drink," replied the ferret.

"That's silly." said Niles, "Rivers don't know if you drink from them." But he wasn't so sure, not here in the Endless Forest.

Frederick looked right at him. "This one knows. You would do better to ask permission." Then he went back to yawning and stretching.

Niles had seen so many strange things already that talking to a river didn't seem as ridiculous as it would have a day before. "Ah, river," he began, "would it be okay with you if I drank a little of your water?"

Now it is one thing to talk to a river, but it is quite another for a river to talk to you. Niles was definitely not expecting to hear a voice from deep within the water. But he did.

"That will be quite alright, little man," the gentle voice replied. "Drink as much as you like. You are quite polite, even if it did take a ferret to tell you the proper way to behave."

"Why not?" thought Niles to himself. "A talking ferret, a talking moose, and now a talking river. I'd love to tell Roger all about them, but he'd never believe me."

"Yes, he would, little man," said the river.

"What? I didn't say anything to you! How did you know ..." Niles was too surprised to even finish his thought.

"I can hear your thoughts," spoke the river softly. "But have no fear, you can trust me. You can trust me as you would trust yourself. If you prefer, I will stop listening until you are ready for me to hear. But tell me, little man, where are you going?"

"I'm on a journey -- a special journey," said Niles. He was unsure exactly how much he should tell the river. He looked to Frederick for guidance, but the ferret was asleep.

"All journeys are special, if you pay attention along the way," said the river. Niles wasn't sure what the river meant, but he thought he would figure it out later. "But which _way_ are you going?"

"How many ways are there?" asked Niles. "There are many ways but only one path," answered the river.

Niles was confused. Talking to the river was fun, and he liked its sparkly voice, but he could make no sense out of the answers. Niles tried a different question. "Do you have a name? I heard Frederick call you the Slow River. Is that really your name?"

"Some call me that," the river responded. "I also have many others, but the oldest one is Itasara, which means 'mighty river'. My father is Old Man River. He flows down from the Mountains of Morning into the Lost Lake. He is older even than I. He just keeps rolling along."

The river's voiced trailed off and Niles was about to ask another question, of which he always had a large supply. But before he could the river continued.

"Remember me while you are on your journey. I will never be far off. If you become tired or discouraged, dip yourself in my waters and I will strengthen you. For I am Itasara, the mighty river, and also Flusso, 'the deepest' and Profondo, 'Queen of the Evening'." After that, the river said no more. Nor did it respond to Niles' questions, but he could sense it was there, and that it was aware of him, and remarkably, that it cared.

As he turned away, a small gust of wind came up and sprayed him with a fine mist of river water. As soon as the droplets hit him, Niles felt energized. There was a strong urge to stay where he was and to let the river "take care of him," but he knew he had to continue his journey. It was getting late.

Still, Niles was loath to leave the banks of Itasara. "Taking a short break would be okay," he thought as he rested his head on a mossy rock. It felt surprisingly soft and firm, like his favorite pillow at home. Niles began to close his eyes.

As sleep crept up on him, Niles started to dream. Not the kind of dream you have when you are fast asleep, but the kind of dream you have when you are very relaxed and not thinking about anything special. He saw Roger and could hear his voice. Roger was telling him "When you start feeling tired, keep going until you feel you cannot go any further, and then take *one* more step. Only then should you sleep."

Niles knew he should go on a bit further, but he probably would have gone to sleep right there by the riverbank had it not been for Frederick.

You may be thinking that Frederick snapped out of his sleep and came over to wake Niles up. But that is not what he did. What the ferret did do was snore. You would not believe that such a small animal could make such noise in his sleep. It not only woke up Niles, it even woke Frederick himself.

"What was that?" the startled ferret asked sleepily.

"It was you," laughed Niles, "snoring loud enough to shake nuts out of the trees."

"Impossible. I don't snore," replied the ferret, pulling himself up to his full height, which wasn't very high after all, and trying to look stern.

"Okay, okay," said Niles. "Whatever it was, I think we need to keep going for a little longer."

And that is how Niles and Frederick ended up walking along the winding soft gravel path until the Sun had completely set and the sky had lost all of its daylight, and until Niles was exhausted. When he felt he was ready to drop, Niles remembered what Roger had said and took *one* more step. It felt good to take *one* more step. He didn't know why, but it seemed to have something to do with completing his journey.

Then a strange thing happened. You probably won't think it so unusual after all of the other experiences that Niles had this first day in the forest. But it was strange, and you will have to admit that when I tell you what it was.

Right in front of Niles, in the middle of this black and white forest, appeared a most comfortable bed. It just appeared, where there was nothing but path and grass and trees a moment before. If that is not strange enough for you, how about this? It was Niles' bed!

Niles was too tired to try to figure out how this was possible. He looked at Frederick, but the ferret was already settling down at the foot of the bed and clearly was going to do nothing but sleep.

What else was there to do but follow the ferret's example? Besides Niles was so tired that he all he wanted now was sleep.

As he took off his shoes, Niles went over the day in his mind. Of course, he remembered meeting Frederick, and Hugh the moose, and the talking river. But he also remembered how familiar things felt differently in the forest. He could feel, hear, smell, and see them. In this black and white world, Niles recalled many colorful experiences -- the shades of the roses, the light dark canopy, and his black, brown, and tan little friend. Black and white could be colorful too, he realized.

As Niles lay on his bed, ready to doze off, he thought he could see stars, even though the trees seemed to block out the sky. He didn't try to figure this out either, but he did start counting the stars. This was a game his dad had taught him when they had gone camping and he had been afraid. He was not afraid now, but it gave him a good feeling to count the twinkling, constant, permanent stars. He felt lighter, almost like he was floating into a restful sleep, with a (softly) snoring ferret warmly cuddled at his feet.

Chapter 9 - Ain't That a Hoot!

Niles could not remember when he had slept better. It seemed he fell asleep one minute and awoke the next, but on arising, he felt rested and refreshed. "How long have I slept?" he wondered. He could see the sky through the branches of the tall trees all around him, and it was a dark shade of black except in the direction where the Sun was rising. There it was a very pale yellow.

"Yellow?" Everything in the Forest (except for Frederick) was black and white. Now the sky was beginning to glow with a distinctly yellow tinge. Not very bright yellow, it's true, but definitely yellow.

Niles practically jumped out of his bed and began to look around. Over towards the river a bunch of daffodils grew. Their petals were a bright yellow. And some of the pebbles on the road had a sparkly look with specks of glittery gold color in them (it was quartz).

Niles began to get excited and looked around for Frederick, but the ferret had gone out on some mission of his own. Then Niles noticed his clothes. He had slept in them all night, but this morning they were fresh and clean, not dusty and wrinkled like when he had fallen asleep. And his bed -- well, his bed was gone. It had disappeared when he wasn't looking. That didn't even faze Niles; after all of the extraordinary things that had
happened in the Forest, a disappearing bed wasn't even worth thinking about!

Besides, Niles was fascinated with the color around him. There are truly thousands of different shades of yellow. It gave the Forest a friendlier feel.

For the first time in his life, Niles was ready to completely enjoy the feel, sounds, smells, and sights of his surroundings. He closed his eyes so he could hear and smell more clearly. Almost immediately he heard his first strange sound of the new day: "Hooooo. Hoot. Hoot. Hoot." (It sounds like an owl -- doesn't it? But in the Endless Forest, who knows?)

Niles opened his eyes and searched for the source of the hooting, looking around rapidly. Nothing moved except for a few leaves rustling in the gentle breeze. As near as he could tell, the sound came from a particularly large tree with old gnarled branches bare of leaves. It stretched out way above him, its arms like crooked fingers pointing towards the ground.

Niles let his sight follow the almost straight tree trunk upwards, dodging the branches that hung to one side or another at regular intervals. The glare of the Sun, now risen well above the horizon, was starting to make it hard to follow the trunk any higher, when suddenly Niles' eyes came to rest on something that was an entirely new shade of yellow. I should say, his eyes came to rest on two things. They were a deep, solid-looking yellow, with a little shine to them, and a black slit down the middle.

With a start, Niles figured out what they were -- they were eyes! *Yellow eyes!*

As is usual when there are two eyes, there was something alive attached to them. In this case, it was the biggest, most beautiful, and also most frightening bird that Niles had ever seen.

It *was* an owl, to be sure, and a grand creature. Niles felt intimidated by its mysterious look, and by its large yellow eyes with their black slits. He had heard stories about owls, most of them evil, and he started to grow afraid. As he did, the yellow eyes of the owl began to grow dimmer and the daffodils turned gray, as if the light of the Sun had suddenly been denied them. Niles could feel Calamidrake stir into life. It swiveled its head around to see what was going on.

Niles wanted to call out for Frederick, but something made him pause. "No," he said to himself in a determined fashion, "I'm going to do this myself. The owl has done nothing to harm me, and its hooting seems happy and friendly. I have no reason to be afraid."

It had actually taken quite a bit of courage for Niles to stand up to his fear in the way he did. After all, it was a really *big* owl. It must have been the right thing to do, however, because the result was immediate. The color returned to the owl's eyes, and the daffodils once more gleamed a brilliant yellow. Calamidrake gave a deep sigh and went back to sleep. Best of all, Frederick popped out of the woods with a grin all over his beautiful black and white and tan face.

Frederick called out to Niles as soon as he saw him. "Look who I found! This is my friend, Henrietta, the Great

Horned Owl. Come closer. Let her take a better look at you."

"I believe I am as close as I want to get," said Niles. Courage was a fine thing, but a dash of caution makes it even better.

The owl quickly took matters into her own hands, or should I say talons, and swooped down from her perch, gliding effortlessly in the morning breeze. Niles was astounded by Henrietta's huge wings, which were much longer than her body, and fascinated by her graceful flight. Just then the owl suddenly folded her wings in towards her body, and dropped almost straight down towards Niles.

He flung up his hands as if to ward off an attack, and then felt a little silly as the owl landed on a branch scarcely five feet about his head. Frederick laughed. But it was a friendly laugh, not at all like the laughs that his classmates had given him that day he climbed the big tree in the schoolyard. Those laughs had made Niles feel bad, but this laugh made him smile inside.

"I believe your little friend is afraid of me, Frederick," Henrietta exclaimed.

"No, I am not," Niles answered. "You startled me a little, and, well, ... I've heard stories about owls." He didn't exactly know how to go on.

Frederick eyed him dubiously and Henrietta just sat and waited. Finally, Niles continued. "You know the stories, with evil owls scaring people and even attacking them. And then you looked kind of scary and your eyes ..."

"How can you think such things about my friend?" the ferret interrupted. "There is nothing evil about Henrietta. Except maybe that she eats all of the best nuts before they fall to the ground where a hungry ferret can get his share." He eyed Henrietta sternly for a brief moment, and then they both laughed. Or really, Frederick laughed and Henrietta gave a kind of rolling hoot something like "hoohoohoohoohoo."

Eventually Henrietta stopped "hooing" long enough to explain. "You see, Frederick, we often judge others by the way they look or things we may have heard. My yellow eyes are different, and Niles has heard stories about wickedness and owls, so Niles was frightened by me and judged me to be evil."

She turned towards Niles and bent her head over to look directly at him. Niles was still uneasy at having the owl stare at him, but when Henrietta talked, people listened. And now she said "once you get to know me, you'll see my yellow eyes as rays of sunshine and not as anything evil."

Niles liked the Great Horned Owl's gentle words and tone. Soon he began to wonder if Henrietta, who seemed both kind and wise, also knew about "you-know-who."

As Niles thought about the Dragon, he even imagined he heard its hiss and felt its hot breath on his neck. Niles started getting red in the face as he usually did when

Calamidrake hissed at him. And as he felt himself getting hot, he noticed Henrietta watching him with those big, yellow, wise eyes.

He thought he saw Henrietta nod before she even said, "Yes, it is a most hideous creature."

It was good to know that Henrietta knew about the Dragon and understood how much he disliked it. This evil-looking (but wise and kind) Great Horned Owl made Niles feel safe. And that was enough to cool Niles' neck and to drown the hiss of the Dragon in a deep pool of understanding, for the time being, at least.

Now Niles felt very good indeed. "I think I can count on that Great Horned Owl to help me if ever I need it," he thought to himself. "In a way, she's like my mother."

No sooner had he thought the word "mother" than a long rumbling laugh came from far off to his left, behind a hill covered with blackberry bushes and a stand of tall rushes. Although he couldn't see it, Niles knew it was the river laughing. Niles felt embarrassed. "Hey," he shouted, "you said you wouldn't listen to my thoughts."

"Sorry," replied the river, still chuckling to itself as it calmly flowed away towards who knows what end.

Niles had little time to dwell on his discomfort, however, since Frederick and Henrietta were making all kinds of noise. Between hoots and chortles (it was the ferret who chortled), Niles could make out only a little of the story the owl was telling.

As soon as they saw him looking on, both of his forest friends turned his way and smiled. "We were just talking about some other children who have been down this path," she explained. "Many have completed their journeys, but some have not." Niles thought he detected a note of sadness in Henrietta's voice when she said "some have not."

"What's so funny about that?" he asked, wondering if the owl was laughing at him.

"Frederick was too," came Calamidrake's voice.

"Just what I don't need now," thought Niles. "Go away," he shouted.

"It's not always that easy," answered the Dragon, starting to shoot steam from both nostrils. Bright red streaks shot outwards from the Dragon's neck, down its legs and through its wings. "You thought they were your friends, but maybe they just wanted to use you for sport. If they think everything you do is funny and stupid, they would be right!"

Frederick came over to Niles and rubbed against his leg. He looked up in concern, but Niles was too involved with Calamidrake to notice.

The truth is that this was more than just another incident between Niles and Calamidrake. The Dragon didn't like the idea of this journey a bit, and it was bent on getting Niles to quit as soon as possible. If it discouraged

Niles enough, he might give up and that would be the end of the journey. Then Calamidrake would have a good chance of gaining control of Niles' mind, possibly forever. So you see it was not just a minor struggle about who was laughing at whom.

Niles didn't know how to reply. As usual, the Dragon had found a way to speak doubts that Niles already felt. The content was very close. Henrietta tried to help.

The Great Horned Owl heard Niles' shout of "Go away." She saw the redness on the boy's neck. Flapping her wings gently, Henrietta glided to a perch on a branch where Niles could easily see her. "We weren't laughing at you," she said gently. "We were laughing at that dumb Dragon. Frederick and I were telling each other stories about the other children, and how they had beaten the Dragon and made _it_ look stupid."

Niles heard Henrietta and he wanted to believe what she said, but Calamidrake was very strong right now. It had turned a brilliant red all over its body, except for a small green spot at the tip of its tail. And it kept shouting at Niles. "Don't believe her. Don't believe her. Just look at that owl. She looks evil, evil, evil! Don't believe anything she says."

Niles was torn. He couldn't make himself believe Henrietta was evil, but he hadn't known her very long. And Calamidrake did make sense. For long seconds the hissing of the Dragon and the soft words of the owl battled in his mind. Even with Henrietta's help, the battle was nearly even.

At that moment a strong breeze sprang up from the direction of the Slow River and carried with it the tiniest amount of fine mist. When the droplets from Itasara touched Niles' hot forehead, it was like an alarm clock waking him up. The Dragon spell was broken in an instant. "How could I ever consider listening to that Dragon!" he exclaimed to himself.

Calamidrake roared in frustration and anger. It whipped its very long tail all the way around its head, making a vicious snapping sound. As the same time, it shot out the greatest cloud of steam it had generated in its entire life.

This was a mistake – a dreadful mistake. The Dragon's timing was bad. Its tail had not quite gotten out of the way before the hot, hot steam hit.

Now if you think the Dragon was roaring before, you should have heard it now. Even the Sun seemed to shake in the sky. Waves of pain and rage overcame Calamidrake. Its brilliant red color faded to a deep blue-gray in a flash, except for the tip of its tail, which was now a glowing scarlet, and would be for a very, very long time.

Niles had reached out his hand towards Henrietta when the Dragon was at its worst, and now the owl sat perched on his right arm. Frederick had wrapped himself around his leg as if to say that nothing would make him let Niles go away. And that was a good thing, for if the Dragon had won that contest (and he came ever so close!) Niles' journey would have been over. Then Niles would have to go through more and worse bad times before he could start another one, if indeed he ever could.

But Calamidrake had lost, thanks to Itasara and to the added strength that Niles had discovered in himself during his first day in the Forest. So now he turned to his two friends and smiled the biggest smile he could ever remember smiling. When they saw the happy expression on his face, they both sighed. Frederick loosened his grip -- a little. Henrietta hooted and shifted her weight from one foot to the other in a kind of owlish dance. "Tell us what happened," they both said at the same time.

And so, Niles told the whole story. When he came to the part about the Dragon burning its own tail, both of his friends starting laughing. They laughed so hard and so long that Niles wondered if they were ever going to stop. But of course, they did, eventually.

"Well, I guess you learned to listen to your friends and not to your enemies," said Frederick between chortles. "But it doesn't take a genius to figure that out."

"I learned a lot more than that," responded Niles. "I thought you were laughing at me, so I began to get angry. That's when the Dragon crept up on me. I should have asked you why you were laughing before I got upset. But I didn't." He stopped suddenly. Another thought had just entered his mind.

Niles turned silent and looked at his friends with a little sadness and embarrassment. "I'm sorry." he said, "I'm really sorry I ever doubted you. I don't ever want to hurt your feelings." There was a trace of a tear in his eye, but Niles brushed it away with the back of his hand.

"It seems you've learned more than one thing today," said Frederick, but then he too because silent and thoughtful.

Henrietta, however, had no intention of slowing down. Still laughing about how the tables had been turned on "Sir Draconis of the Ugly Thoughts," she spied a large branch on a huge walnut tree that overlooked the path. With an owlish chuckle, she flew to this new perch and jumped up and down on it as fast as she could. The immediate result was a great shower of walnuts out of the tree and onto the heads of Frederick and Niles below. "Here are some of those nuts you're always complaining about," she hooted at Frederick.

Chapter 10 - The Dawn of Wisdom

The day had dawned beautifully cool; Calamidrake was soon forgotten. Niles looked forward to a wonderful day with his friends, but even in the Endless Forest things eventually come to an end. Before he knew it, Henrietta was telling Niles that she had to attend to business somewhere else and Frederick was waving good bye to the owl.

Looking up, Niles watched Henrietta fly gracefully away, soaring on unseen drafts with only the slightest of effort. The stars were no longer visible in the slowly brightening sky. The roof of the forest was covered by a canopy that was not deep black, but rather a lighter shade of dark. Somehow it fit Niles' mood. "It's like a blanket keeping me safe," he thought. He cleared his mind of worries and forgot about the Dragon - for a time.

Shouldering his backpack, Niles started off down the path again, Frederick at his side. The ferret was in a playful mood, dashing from side to side on the path, and sometimes running complete circles around Niles. All the while Frederick was singing little phrases of nothing like "it's good, it's jive, to be alive," and "we'll have fun, fun, fun 'til daddy ..." Niles could not understand the last part of that song. "Until Daddy does what?" he questioned himself. It sounded like something about a Tea Bird. Whatever that was.

The high spirits of his traveling companion reminded Niles of his own good times with Roger. Soon Niles too began to feel free. Each step brought new delights. It was as of he was floating through the air, but at the same time the ground was beneath him, hard and soft. It steadied him somewhat, but without taking away his freedom. It was an amazing feeling - to be safe and free at the same time!

"Maybe this is what the journey is all about," he thought to himself. At the same time he knew there was much more to it. An iciness touched his heart. He wondered just where he was going and what would be left of him when it was over.

Idly putting his hand into his pocket, Niles felt something hard and smooth and cool. He pulled out his lucky stone and held it in the palm of his hand. "Could this have had any part in vanquishing Calamidrake?" he wondered. To be sure he didn't lose it, Niles pushed the stone securely to the bottom of his pocket, underneath some tissues and an old candy bar wrapper that usually lived there (except when his mother emptied his pockets before doing the laundry).

"It's like you and Henrietta, and even the river," he began, looking over his shoulder to where Frederick had been turning somersaults.

"What's like me?" came Frederick's voice from behind a bush. The ferret was trying to hold the woody stalks apart so that he could get at some nuts that had fallen beneath.

"My lucky stone," answered Niles.

"Thanks a lot," retorted Frederick. "It's nice to be compared to a rock."

Calamidrake snickered, but Niles paid no attention and it quickly shriveled up and disappeared again.

"I didn't mean it like that," Niles laughed. "It just that my lucky stone will be here when I need it, just like my friends in the forest. Like you, and like Henrietta, and like the Slow River."

Frederick scowled. He wasn't really angry, of course. He was just having fun with Niles. "Like a rock," he muttered and slunk away under a smaller bush, between two young trees, over a small hill and then who knows where. But secretly he was touched, and from that day on Frederick never forgot Niles' lucky stone.

The morning of the second day of the journey spun away. The path led Niles through glens of white-barked aspen trees and fragrant pines, across a field of yellow daisies with black centers (they were Black-Eyed Susans, Frederick told him later), and past a small brook that ran swiftly away towards the river.

Niles' backpack felt lighter than before. He had eaten a number of sandwiches, and had shared as many with the always-hungry ferret, but that didn't account for all of the change. "Maybe I'm just get stronger," thought Niles.

"You surely are, little man," came a gentle voice off to his right.

Gottlieb, The Endless Forest

"The river," Niles said to himself, "listening to my thoughts again." And somehow, he didn't mind this time. He was beginning to trust Itasara.

"Thank you," came the voice again, "but it is really yourself that you are beginning to trust."

"I never know exactly what you mean," said Niles aloud, "but what you say gives me a good feeling inside." He would have continued, because, as usual, he had lots of questions to ask, but he could hear the river tumbling and turning away into the dimming depths of the forest, and he knew that he would get no answers. At least not right now.

Full of energy, Niles looked forward to his journey and to new experiences. When he had started he was afraid of anything unknown. He had worried about when the Dragon would pop up and spoil things. But not now.

Now let me tell you, it is one thing to be happy and energetic, but it is another to be careless and to fail to look out for pratfalls and pits and other sorts of nasty things. Sorry to say, Niles was beginning to get over-confident and that can lead to a lack of caution and that can lead to all kinds of problems. Niles was not watching for them, but the hard spots in life's road do not go away for being ignored. I am afraid Niles will find that out for himself -- but not just yet.

Simply put, Niles was happy. Frederick was back, running and walking and skipping ahead of Niles, and sometimes behind Niles and often to the right or left, and once or twice, even _above_ Niles, hanging from an overhanging branch as Niles walked by. "Lead on, little friend," Niles thought happily. But it was now he, Niles, who was leading. "That must mean something," he thought. But he didn't know what.

Niles was thinking smiling thoughts about his good friend Roger and other boys that he liked (but no girls, at least none he would admit to). His imagination led him along the grassy paths near his home, past the ball field and Mrs. Greenstem's garden full of flowers ("We can fix that," came a naughty thought), and to his own warm and welcoming home.

And that's how Niles came to think about his parents, and that's when he realized they would be missing him. He could almost see his Mom, with her kind eyes and her ready smile, and of course her hugs. He thought of his father's playful grin and wise eyes, and he imagined himself playing the clever games Dad made up for him. As he thought of his parents, he began to feel sad.

Maybe that's what gave Calamidrake its chance. Before Niles knew what was happening, it had weaseled its way back into his thoughts, saying that he was a bad son who had deserted his parents. He could feel the angry thoughts beginning, and he became irritated.

"Go away, Dragon", he practically shouted. And the Dragon did.

But this time it left in a strange way. It didn't fade slowly away, or curl up and hide in his tail. Instead, it popped. It was there one moment, and then "Pop!" it was gone. Niles realized that this was another way to rid himself of Calamidrake, but it didn't feel right and the Dragon didn't seem very far away.

Chapter 11 - Just Grin and "Bear" it

The day had begun to turn cloudy. The soft breeze that usually sighed through the trees had turned into a stronger wind, somewhat threatening, tossing the treetops back and forth. Niles had put his parents out of his mind but he still felt uncomfortable. The path was now clothed in a deep shadow from a passing cloud, as Niles walked slowly down it, kicking stones.

The strange disappearance of the Dragon worried him. Even the sound of his shoe hitting a stone reminded him of the "Pop" the Dragon made when it had disappeared. He kicked another pebble ("pop"), and then a larger one ("POP!"). This last went bouncing along the path with a skitter and a scatter, until finally it skipped off the path to his right, and disappeared under a small bush. To Niles' great surprise, a small cry rang out from where the stone had landed.

He had never thought that kicking could hurt stones, but then this was the Endless Forest, and many strange things happened here. So he stopped kicking because he didn't want to cause pain even to a rock, but after just another ten steps, he began to get curious. He wasn't sure he had heard a cry after all; maybe it had just been a gust of the freshening wind causing an old tree branch to bend and creak.

"I'll just try once more," Niles thought, as he came across a particularly large pebble in the middle of the path. He gave it a very little kick. The stone rolled two or three feet along the path and came to rest. Carefully, Niles approached the pebble again and kicked it a little harder. This time it bounced once, deflected to the left, hit off a sapling at the side of the path, and fell back right in the middle of the path.

"I knew it," said Niles aloud, "stones don't cry," and he gave the large pebble a kick as hard as he could. It skipped along the path, bouncing from side to side and then, with a large hop, leapt over a bush and disappeared. And then it gave a cry, somewhat louder than before.

Niles was astonished. Perhaps he should try to find the stone among the bushes. In fact, he was just about to begin searching when a tiny movement at the very corner of his vision, attracted his attention. What Niles saw almost made him jump out of his skin; in fact, he probably would have, but his skin was so firmly attached to his body that when Niles jumped, his skin just jumped with him.

You might wonder what could startle Niles so. After all, he had already been surprised by a talking ferret, a huge moose, an evil-looking owl, and a mind-reading river! By now, Niles should be ready for anything. But he wasn't. Not for this.

Standing directly in front of Niles, squarely in the middle of the path, clothed in nothing but deep shadows (and one stray sunbeam that defied the clouds to shine on its face) was a very, very, very big brown bear. Standing upright on two legs, it dominated the path, and it looked upset.

Niles didn't stop to stare, he didn't cry out, he didn't even think. He just dove head-first off the path and behind the first bush he could find. I certainly would not call Niles a coward for hiding. He was taken completely by surprise, and this was a very big bear, and everyone knows bears can be dangerous, and this was the Endless Forest where anything could happen, and Frederick was nowhere to be seen. When Niles told the story later, he would say that he was just being careful, but truthfully "terrified" comes closer to the mark.

There is nothing wrong with being afraid, so long as you keep your wits about you. And to his credit, Niles did. No sooner had he hit the ground, his backpack breaking free and lodging against the base of a small tree, than Niles started to think. First, he needed to see what the bear was doing. Was it looking for him? Worse yet, did it know where he was and was it preparing to attack? Cautiously, Niles parted the branches of the bush above him and peered out.

And there was the bear, still on the path, still standing on two legs, and looking his way. He had something in his paws. Was it a rock? Did bears in the Endless Forest throw stones?

Niles blinked his eyes and strained to see what the bear was holding. As he got used to the shadows, everything came into sharp focus. Niles could only stare in disbelief. Even in the Endless Forest, an eight-foot-tall bear carrying a flower pot with a plant growing out of it was out of the ordinary.

Yet that was what Niles saw. The bear was holding the pot very gently in one paw, and was shaking the other paw vigorously, all the while whimpering softly. Niles' fears melted away. He could not be afraid of an animal that held a beautiful flower so tenderly. Besides, the bear seemed to be crying. Maybe he needed help.

Once again Niles showed that he could be as brave as anyone when the situation demanded it. Leaving the shelter of his bush, shaking off the dirt, and tucking his shirt back into his pants, Niles walked slowly towards the bear.

"A stone hit me here -- on my tender spot," said the bear in a most pitiful voice. Niles immediately felt an unbearable pain in his elbow, and realized that he was feeling what the bear felt. With no further thought for his own safety, he ran up to the bear. "Oh, I'm sorry, I'm sorry," he cried. "I never meant to hurt anyone. How can I help?"

"Here, hold Morning Gloria," said the bear, handing Niles the potted plant.

Niles reached out and took the flower carefully. She was lovely, even in the shadowed forest. A single strong stem quickly branched in several directions. Leaves grew in clumps of three from little side stems. Just above each group of leaves, a small flower appeared. The flowers were closed tightly, not yet ready to bloom, and Niles couldn't tell what color they would be.

Meanwhile, the bear sat down and rubbed his foot. "Is that infernal Dragon chasing you?" he asked.

Niles was amazed. "You know about him too?"

"Oh yes, everyone in this forest knows about that scoundrel," said the bear.

"But have you ever met him personally? Have you actually _seen_ him?" asked Niles.

"That I have, more than once. But since I found Morning Gloria, not so often anymore."

A rustle of branches from a low-lying bush attracted Niles's attention, and just then Frederick peeked a furry little head out from under the lowest of them. "Oh, I see you've met Victorious," the ferret exclaimed, scampering over to Niles.

Niles thought "Yes, I have, and it would have been nice if we had met him _together_," but he didn't say that. He could hardly expect the ferret to spend every moment following a boy around. Ferrets had to find food, and do other things. It was the "other things" that had Niles just the slightest bit worried. What exactly was Frederick doing when he went off by himself?

"You must have been frightened," Frederick continued. "Victorious was once the most restless and combative bear in the forest. He could be a fast friend. Always had a good heart. But he played too rough. Most of us stayed well clear of him, whenever we could. Then one day, he showed up holding a flower in a pot. He named her Morning Gloria, and his restlessness went away. Since then, Victorious has been the best of friends to everyone he meets."

The ferret paused. This was an extraordinarily long speech for him. He would much rather crack nuts than talk. But I think Frederick felt a little bit guilty about being away when Niles and Victorious met.

Niles didn't wait for the ferret to start talking again. He had already thought of at least ten questions to ask Victorious. He was certainly very good at thinking up questions, was Niles. He started off with the one I would have picked: "How did you find Morning Gloria?"

Victorious was now sitting on the forest floor next to the path, gently rubbing his elbow. He looked up at Niles in a not unkindly fashion, breathed a long sigh, and began: "It's a long story and an old story. Are you sure you want to hear it?"

"Oh, I would love to hear your story," said Niles, sitting down on the ground next to the huge bear. He put Morning Gloria down softly, between them, and the bear slipped its paw gently around the pot. Frederick stopped searching for nuts and lay down at Niles' feet. He knew the story well but loved to here it told anyway.

"It was a day like any other," said Victorious, and then he paused. "It's a long story, are you absolutely sure you want to hear it?" he asked.

"Yes," shouted Niles and Frederick at the same time. "Go on already," continued the ferret. "I really like the story, especially the part where ..."

"Whoa, little friend. Let me tell it then," interrupted Victorious. And so he began his tale.

> It happened on a day like any other.
> We went to take a drink, me and my brother.
> We sat upon the banks of Itasara --
> The two of us and neighbors Jean and Farah.
> We gazed upon the water clear and cool,
> And drank from time to time from Sparkling Pool.

Here he looked at Niles closely. Niles just smiled and nodded and then whispered to Frederick: "Does Victorious always speak in rhymes?"

"Not always," answer the ferret. "And don't encourage him. He thinks he's a poet. If he tells the whole story in rhyme, we'll be here for a week."

Victorious went right on. "Then, out of nowhere, came this most hideous creature, a creature with two heads." He had stopped rhyming. Perhaps he had overheard the whispered conversation between Niles and Frederick, but more likely he had come to the part of the story where the "creature" appears. Evil and poetry do not mix well on the tongues of good people (or good animals).

"Two heads!" gasped Niles. He had never heard of a creature with two heads, not even in the Endless Forest.

"Well," said Victorious, "it didn't exactly have two heads, but rather two faces."

"Two faces! How can you have two faces and not have two heads?" exclaimed Niles.

"I see you want to be exact," continued Victorious. "Well, this creature really did not have two faces, but was rather two-faced. That would be the precise way to put it."

Meanwhile Frederick had inched closer to the bear, swishing his tail back and forth, and brushing Victorious' paw with each swing. The bear didn't seem to mind. "Come on, already," he said impatiently, "get to the good part, where you ..."

"I'm getting there. I'm getting there," laughed Victorious. And indeed, he was, but with some people (and with some animals too), getting somewhere can take a long time, even when they are not talking in rhyme. Seeing that trying to hurry the bear would do no good, Frederick settled down, produced a few nuts from somewhere, and started cracking one.

Victorious slid over to a particularly comfortable looking tree trunk and rested his considerable bulk against it. A sunbeam broke through the canopy of trees and shone on the forest floor right in the middle of Niles, Frederick, and Victorious, where Morning Gloria lay. Feeling the warmth, the plant's leaves stretched open and turned towards the Sun, but her flowers stayed tightly curled and did not open.

Chapter 12 - Will the Bear Take the Dare?

Meanwhile, Niles was really confused. "Two heads, two faces, two-faced! What does it all mean?" he thought. He glanced up at Victorious' brown face as if to ask, but the bear didn't seem to notice and just went on with his story.

"This two-faced thing started laughing at me in front of my brother and neighbors and all of the other Forest creatures. It said I was big but that I was afraid of everything. 'Why,' it said, 'you're probably even too afraid to walk across that little stream.'

"I looked at it and thought that it was pretty big for a stream. Yes, it was really a small river, since you like to have things stated exactly." Here Victorious glanced down at Niles, but he had a kind smile on his face.

"It wasn't very deep and there were plenty of flat dry stones to step on. I wouldn't even have to get my paws wet. I certainly wasn't afraid of crossing the river, and I was just about to tell the creature so when it began to laugh again.

"'Come on, come on', it snapped impatiently. 'Will you or won't you?'

"'Of course, I will,' I answered. 'It's easy.'

"'Easy?' it replied. 'Too easy perhaps? Well, let's make it a little harder. You can only step on the white rocks. How's that?'

"I looked at the river and saw that about half of the rocks were white. There will still enough of them for me to cross, but it would be a little harder, and I might get my toes wet once or twice. 'It's still easy,' I said and started to put my foot on the first rock.

"'Of course you'll do it on one foot,' interrupted the two-faced creature.

"Well, that gave me pause, but the creature kept laughing and yelling 'I dare you. I dare you.' Now, I would have to _hop_ from rock to rock, and that would be hard. Very hard. But by now I was so mad that I didn't even think. I just picked up my left foot and hopped right out onto that first rock. I figured I had to get started right away or else that creature would think up some more nasty little conditions.

Niles understood dares very well. Many times, the children at school had dared him to do things, and many times he had taken the dares. Usually, it turned out badly. Niles knew Victorious was headed for trouble. At least someone was enjoying this part of the story; unfortunately, it was Calamidrake, who chortled, grinned, and blew three huge smoke rings.

Niles ignored the Dragon. He felt close to the bear; he understood how Victorious felt. "It's just like me and

Calamidrake," he thought. "Poor Victorious. He was trapped."

"Yes, I was," said the bear, inclining his head towards Niles, but looking straight ahead into the forest.

This startled Niles a little, because he hadn't said anything out loud. "Do all forest creatures read minds?" he asked.

"No, we don't read minds," Victorious replied. "We are all connected and can imagine what others think and feel if we listen with a third ear." Hmm, here he was, Victorious, getting weird with the third ear, but Niles got it.

Niles knew that both he and Victorious had taken dares and gotten into trouble. And even if they had not shared the same experiences, Victorious could imagine what others might think and feel about certain situations. And, at that moment, Niles realized that he, too, could understand where Victorious was coming from, even though they might not have had the exact same journey. This felt good to Niles. If you would have asked him how he felt, he would have said "part of something bigger than me." "Yes, that is the feeling we get from being empathic and connected to others," whispered Itasara, so quietly, that Niles thought he might have imagined it-but he did not. Niles felt powerful. "Victorious and me," he thought, "or is it 'Victorious and I'? We could have handled any two-faced creature if we did it together!"

And that reminded him of a question of course. "What does two-faced mean, anyway?" he asked in general.

Frederick answered. "It means someone who says one thing and really means something different."

That didn't completely satisfy Niles, but at least it gave him some idea. A "two-faced" creature didn't actually have two faces. It was like smiling with one face but having another hidden face that was frowning. He pondered this for a moment, but soon his attention was drawn back to Victorious, who was rubbing the side of his head and staring sadly into the Forest.

"So, what happened?" Niles wanted to know.

"What do you think happened?" Victorious answered. "I started crossing the river, hopping from one white stone to the next. Everything seemed to be going well until the middle of the stream. My foot landed on the side of a rock. I slipped and started to fall. To catch myself, I had to put my other foot down into the river.

"I should have stopped then, but the two-faced creature laughed, and I was determined to go on. I steadied myself and took the next hop. This was onto a much larger stone, and one that was very flat, so I had no trouble. In fact, I had almost reached the far side when I came to a really hard part. The next white stone was just about as far away as I could hop, and it wasn't very big. I should have stopped then, but of course I didn't. I just took a deep breath and hopped as far as I could." Victorious paused for a moment. Niles held his breath.

"And I made it!" continued the bear abruptly. Niles broke into a smile.

"Almost," concluded Victorious.

"Uh, oh," thought Niles, no longer grinning.

"That's when I stepped on it."

"Stepped on what?" asked Niles, who could hardly contain himself. This was a really interesting story.

"Why, Mr. Stonefish," said Victorious.

"Mr. Stonefish!" exclaimed Niles. "Aren't stonefish poisonous?"

"Yes," continued Victorius, "they are, and in this case also very upset. He was so angry at being stepped on (and you can hardly blame him) that he gave me an extra dose of poison. I began to feel dizzy, but I managed to stumble my way to the bank of the river. And then I fell and hit my head on a tree trunk." He began rubbing the side of his head again, as if to show Niles where it had been injured, but Niles couldn't see anything there. Probably it had already healed, but there are some pains you never forget, even when they are actually gone.

"I didn't remember anything else until the next morning. The stonefish poison is very serious, especially when you get an extra dose, but it wasn't enough to kill me. So when dawn broke over the Forest, I woke up. I was lying in a bed of soft grass where my friends must have put me, and a blanket covered my toes that sometimes get cold at night. But my foot was still swollen and painful, and my head ached where it had hit the tree. And that wasn't the worst part.

"Where did your friends go?" asked Niles. "Why didn't they stay to make sure you were going to be alright?"

"I am sure they did, at least until they knew I would recover. Then they left me alone. They knew I would not want to face them after the stupid thing I had done.

"I was terribly depressed. How could I have taken an idiotic dare like that? What must all of my Forest friends think of me now?" Victorious looked towards Frederick. The ferret was busy digging the last bits of meat from his final nut, but he was still paying close attention. When the bear stopped talking, Frederick looked up. He was about to break in and begin telling the rest of the tale himself. Victorious, noticing this, chuckled and went on quickly.

"I felt stupid and humiliated. I didn't even think I could keep on living in the Forest among all of the animals who had been my friends. I just lay there on the ground with my eyes closed, thinking sad thoughts."

"How long I would have stayed there, I don't know, but a raindrop fell right on my nose. I shook my head to make it fall off." Victorious paused for just a moment. If he had stopped for any longer, Frederick would surely have interrupted because this was his favorite part.

"It was then I saw her. Morning Gloria. I had almost fallen right on top of her, and in fact one of her stems was bent and trapped under my side. This was back when I was still a restless bear, and I sometimes did dumb things like taking dares. I even got into fights once in a while, but I never liked hurting anything. So as soon as I noticed that I was bending one of her stems, I rolled over to set her free. Then I got up and shook myself off. I wanted to make sure I hadn't hurt her. She was the most beautiful plant I had ever seen.

Niles looked at Morning Gloria, now nestled in her pot just a few feet from him. She was pretty, but the "most beautiful plant"? He didn't think so. Daffodils were brighter and roses were more colorful and honeysuckle smelled sweeter. "Maybe bears see things differently," he thought.

"We do," said Victorious. Once again, he somehow knew what Niles was thinking. And then he broke into poetry.

"But never have you seen her fair at dawn,
    When all her flowers break their nightly sleep.
    Each one pale blue like daytime sky is drawn,
    With centers round, perfection white and deep.

The clustered blooms in starlets of dark green,
Soft leaves of silken shadow treasure's seat.
And, Oh! their fragrance, delicate and clean,
In cold prevails and withers not in heat.

Through all the morning shares she with the world
Her beauty and her being and her song.
Then when the Sun ascends, her petals curled
She weaves into their hidden pattern strong.
The leaves fold o'er them like a curtain drawn -
A bed of rest until the coming dawn."

Everyone's eyes were on Morning Gloria, who was waving her leaves gently in the breeze. Calamidrake apparently didn't like this part of the story, because it was struggling to hide itself as completely as possible in its own tail.

Niles was very impressed with Victorious. Who would have thought that a forest bear could write such poetry!

"That's a sonnet," Frederick announced proudly.

"A sonnet? What's that?" asked Niles.

Apparently, Frederick could recognize a sonnet, but he really didn't know what one was, so Victorious had to answer. "A sonnet is a special kind of poem. We had a boy here in the Forest once, so the old tales tell. He wrote a lot of them. What was his name? Let me think ... William, I recall. William Shake-something.

"He was always making up poems, and even when he wasn't reciting them, he spoke like a poem. Very strange. I remember one time my brother and I were gathering honey. At almost the same moment, we both got stung. Neither of us saw what did it, but it was probably bees. Of course, it could have been wasps or hornets or even horseflies. It wasn't much of a story, but William made a big deal out of it.

"'Two bees or not two bees? That is the question.' That was how he put it. Very strange."

To be honest, Niles was not terribly interested in sonnets or William Shake-something. He *was* fascinated by Morning Gloria. At the first break in Victorious' explanation, he asked a different question. "Doesn't she talk?" (by now Niles was used to everything in Forest having a voice.)

"I don't know," answered Victorious. "She's never spoken to me. But her magic is different. When you see her at dawn, as you first wake up, you are filled with hope. You realize that it's a new day, and that you can do anything you set your mind to, no matter what has gone before. The past doesn't disappear, but it does lose its ability to bind you.

"On that first day I looked at her and understood many things. The first was that I had stepped on poor Mr. Stonefish and that I should apologize. He was sorry too; he wouldn't have released his poison if he had known that it was I.

"But I also understood that I wouldn't have hurt him if I had not taken that idiotic dare.

"But you didn't do it on purpose," interrupted Niles.

"No, I didn't," responded the bear, "but because I did something dangerous, someone else got hurt. Actually, two some ones got hurt -- Mr. Stonefish *and* Morning Gloria. I had nearly broken off the stem that was trapped under my side and it hung over, touching the ground and looking so sad.

"You should know," Victorious continued, looking meaningfully at Niles, "that when you listen to two-faced creatures and do the things they tell you, other people get hurt too."

Niles did know. It had happened often enough to him.

Victorious didn't give Niles much time to get sad. "I knew I needed to help her somehow," the bear went on. "Fortunately, I remembered where I had stored a honey pot and it was not too far away. I ran through the Forest as fast as my legs would carry me to the trunk of an old fallen tree where bees had a hive, and where I stored my honey. There was the pot, full of honey of course. I gobbled down that honey as quickly as I could."

Victorious looked down at Frederick with a slightly guilty look on his face. "You wouldn't want me to waste it, would you?" he cried.

"Of course not," Niles answered for the ferret. Actually, he didn't have an opinion as to whether the bear should have stopped to eat the honey or not; but he sensed that Victorious would feel better if he said it, and, also, he wanted the storytelling to go on.

"So, I emptied the pot and ran to a nearby brook where I washed the pot out and then I ran back to Morning Gloria. Carefully, I dug into the ground around her, being sure not to harm her roots. Soon I had separated a ball of soil with all of Morning Gloria in it. It was just the right size for my pot. Gently, I put her into the pot and carried her down to the Slow River. I showed her to Itasara and asked what to do. The broken stem was still bent over and its leaves were beginning to wilt. Even the healthy stems were starting to bend.

"Itasara said nothing for long minutes. Her waters just flowed by and I was about to give up when a small green frog came by and jumped up onto the flower pot. A few drops of water fell off of him into the soil in the pot. At once, Morning Gloria began to perk up. I could see her stems straighten a little."

"That was it! I needed to give her water. I asked Itasara if I could but the river still didn't answer. 'Forgive me, Itasara,' I said, 'but I have to do this.' I put my paw in the water and sprinkled some gently on Morning Gloria. I kept doing this until all of her stems looked straight and strong, even the injured one. A few drops of water dripped out of the bottom of the pot, so I knew I had given her enough.

"As I turned away from the river, carrying Morning Gloria carefully in both hands, Itasara finally spoke. 'Good work,' she said.

"'You're here!' I exclaimed a little peevishly. 'Why didn't you answer me before?'

'I didn't have to,' the river answered. 'You knew what to do yourself; you didn't need me to tell you.'

"Of course, she was right," continued Victorious. "I had learned a lot that morning, but the most important was that I could rely on myself. I didn't need any advice from a two-faced creature; I didn't have to take dares and get into fights because it told me to. And I never have again."

"What a great story!" said Niles enthusiastically, barely waiting for Victorious to finish his last sentence. "So, the two-faced creature was gone forever."

"Forever?" responded Victorious. "No, not forever certainly. And since you like to be precise, not really 'gone' either."

Niles was puzzled. "But you said you never listened to it again."

"That's right," answered the bear. "I never listened to it again, but that doesn't mean it was gone. It had just lost its power over me because I had learned enough about myself to control it. I had grown. I was strong. I was strong enough so that I didn't have to prove it by fighting.

"That's why the two-faced creature is powerless. It still talks to me, and I hear what it says. That's useful to me because it helps me understand what I'm feeling. But I don't do what it tells me because, like Itasara said, I know what to do myself."

Niles was very impressed. He looked at Victorious in awe. "That's wonderful," he said. "And it's kind of like Calamidrake, my Dragon."

"You dummy," interjected Frederick, who had been rummaging around at the base of a bush, "the two-faced creature _is_ your Dragon."

"Well," said Victorious, "it is _MY_ Dragon, if you want to be precise."

Chapter 13 - Mice are Nice

Niles spent most of the next hour or two putting the morning's experiences away in his mind. Others knew about the Dragon -- that he had already figured out -- but he had always thought that the Dragon actually appeared only in his own mind and maybe in his friend Roger's. Now he realized that even forest creatures had their own Dragon. Maybe everybody had one!

While Niles was adjusting his mind (you would say he was daydreaming), Frederick had also made a discovery. Just a few steps away there was a small hill with a crown of beautiful white aspen trees. Below the aspens were dark and ragged old walnut and tall majestic pecan trees. When a strong wind blew, the trees shed their nuts, which bounded and pranced and leapt and skidded until many of them came to rest under a Gather bush.

Now Gather bushes like to grow in low spots and lots of interesting things can be found underneath them. The ferret knew this, and that's why he poked around underneath the one that grew just off the path. That's how he found a huge pile of walnuts and pecans, so I don't need to tell you what he was going to do for the next hour. Or maybe two.

Victorious had already left. Telling the story had reminded the bear about honey, and honey had reminded him that he was hungry, and being hungry reminded him of a low ridge on the other side of the aspen-covered hill.

That's where berry bushes grew, and they were just beginning to ripen. He would be back in an hour. Or maybe two.

Niles was alone in the forest as morning gave way to noon, and noon to early afternoon. The Sun was already beginning to drop lower in the sky when Niles realized that he hadn't eaten all day. He thought about the nuts that Frederick was eating, but he didn't want to crawl under the Gather bush. There was no telling what might be hiding there, and besides, he wasn't sure how the ferret would feel about sharing his lunch. (Frederick would have been happy to, but he didn't know that Niles liked nuts.)

Niles didn't know that Victorious was a short way off feasting on blackberries, blueberries, raspberries, and purple sodaberries, a kind which grew only in the Endless Forest.

All Niles could think of to eat was peanut butter and jelly sandwiches, and, to be frank, he was getting tired of them. Still, they were better than nothing. He decided to make one Frederick's way, with the peanut butter in the middle. He had never tried one like that before; it might be good. At least it would be different.

In fact, it turned out to be surprisingly good! It tasted the same, to be sure, but with the peanut butter in the middle the jelly didn't keep squirting out of the sandwich and onto his clothes.

He was just cleaning up from lunch and wondering where he might get some water to drink when Victorious returned. His face was stained with juice and he had paws full of some kind of purple berry.

"Try these," he said, handing the berries to Niles. "They're sodaberries. Very tasty. I'm going to the river to wash my face."

"Wait," shouted Niles. "I'm coming with you. I'm thirsty." He scrambled to his feet, which is not as easy as it sounds with both hands full of sodaberries. Try it if you don't believe me. If you don't have sodaberries, use something that won't make too much of a mess when you drop it.

Somehow Niles managed to get up without dropping more than a few berries. He stumbled awkwardly off after the bear. Popping a berry into his mouth whenever he got a chance, juice dripping down his chin and staining his shirt purple, he kept mumbling "Boy, these are really good!"

"Pop" went a sodaberry as he put a particularly big one in his mouth. They did that from time to time. They were kind of fizzy and bubbly, like soda. The popping sound reminded Niles of something, but he couldn't remember exactly what it was. That was just as well because he wasn't quite ready to deal with it yet.

The river wasn't far away, and it took Victorious and Niles only a few minutes to reach it. The bank here was a gentle grassy slope. Large willow trees grew in abundance. Their graceful leaves, gray in the shadows, very nearly touched the water. Occasionally, a small yellow flower dropped from the trees and floated gently off down the river on some secret forestly mission.

Victorious stepped up to the river first, since Niles was still a little shy around her. "Hello, Itasara. We've come to wash and drink, if you don't mind."

"Certainly," came the reply, half whispered and half sung. "It is a lovely day and the Glen of Discovery is a perfect place for friends to meet. Stay for a while. Henrietta's coming."

That sounded great to Niles. He would love to see the owl again. "Glen of Discovery" sounded promising too. But then he remembered Frederick. "I have to go back," he said. "My friend Frederick is waiting and he won't know where we are."

"No, you don't" came a voice from somewhere. It sounded like the ferret, but had a strange echoing quality to it. Niles looked around but found no trace of his friend.

"Frederick?" he questioned. "Where are you?"

"In here," came the voice, growing louder. In just a moment, the familiar ferret head appeared out of a hole in the ground near the base of one of the largest willow trees. Frederick was looking around in all directions, licking his lips with his cute gray tongue and looking very satisfied.

"Have you been hunting nuts again?" Niles laughed.

"Well, no," said the ferret, a little embarrassed. "Ferrets don't live on just nuts."

Niles didn't know, so he asked. "What else do you eat?"

That might have been a little impolite because Frederick didn't answer right away, except to stammer "er, ah, er," and things like that.

"Mice," came a voice from high above. "Just like me." It was Henrietta speaking as she swept down along the river with a few slow beats of her powerful wings. She glided to a perch on a slender branch of a small oak tree just a few feet from where Niles stood.

"Mice!" exclaimed Niles. He wasn't thinking very clearly right now, having been startled by the owl whose approach he hadn't heard. If he had taken time to think before he spoke, Niles wouldn't have exclaimed "Yech!" That was definitely impolite. Frederick clearly didn't like it and Henrietta beat her wings back and forth a few times, as if she was going to fly away.

"What's wrong with that?" scowled the ferret. "We eat mice. You eat peanut butter and jelly. Berries too from the look of your face. We eat nuts and mice."

All Niles could think of to say was "But you ate peanut butter and jelly too and you liked it!"

"Maybe you would like mice, too, if you tried them," replied Frederick a little bit testily.

Niles thought for a minute. There was no way he was going to eat mice, but he wanted to be careful not to offend his friends. The owl was watching him carefully, her yellow eyes narrowed. Actually, the owl was only protecting her eyes from the brightness of the Sun, which had just broken through the clouds. But Niles didn't know that and he thought she might be angry.

To make sure he didn't make his friends feel badly, Niles thought carefully before he answered: "Well, I'm very full right now. Maybe later when I'm hungry again."

Henrietta chuckled. "I saw you crossing your fingers," she said. "And, no, I'm not angry. You are welcome to mice. I will even catch them for you since I doubt if you know how. But you needn't try them if you don't want to.

Niles was relieved. "Well," he began, "it's just that I tried a peanut butter and jelly sandwich made Frederick's way -- with the peanut butter inside -- and it was good. So I thought maybe I should try this too." He looked very doubtful though, because the thought of eating mice, particularly uncooked mice, was not a pleasant one.

Now Henrietta really laughed and Frederick and Victorious joined in. Even Itasara sent little wavelets against the shore, making a "slap, slap, slap" sound. Niles was confused. He had tried to be nice and now everyone was laughing at him.

"Don't be upset," Henrietta said soothingly, when she could get any words out between chuckles. "We're not making fun of you. That was very noble, offering to eat mice just to please your friends."

Niles was thinking that he hadn't actually offered to eat mice; he had just said "maybe" and that was with his fingers crossed. But he got no further along this line of thought.

"You don't need to do everything I do," Henrietta continued. "Pick out those things that seem right to you and try them. That will help you to learn and to grow. But don't try to be exactly like me. After all, you are Niles and I am Henrietta."

These words seemed to be very wise, even though Niles didn't completely understand them. Of course, he was Niles and she was Henrietta. Those were their names. But clearly the owl had meant more. Perhaps it was that each person should be strong enough to decide what to do by himself. That was probably it. And Niles did feel a lot stronger now.

If was a relief in any case. He wouldn't have to eat mice. "Yech!" he thought, but this time he didn't say it aloud. Itasara laughed.

Chapter 14 - The "Pop" Won't Stop

Grey clouds mostly hid the Sun, but a single beam escaped, and, breaking through the canopy of willow branches, highlighted the carpet of fur that covered Victorious' broad brown back.

Niles lay on the ground, watching lazily as the leaves swayed back and forth, moved by the wind or perhaps by an unknown force peculiar to this Glen of Discovery. The earth felt both dry and moist at the same time, by which I mean that it was wet enough to feel cool but not so wet as to soak into his clothes.

His gaze fell upon Victorious. Niles appreciated the huge bear; Victorious was truly a handsome animal, with lovely rich brown fur -- except on his belly, where it was much lighter. It was only at this very moment that Niles realized that something had changed. You have probably already noticed it, but Niles had been busy with other things, such as eating purple sodaberries and avoiding eating mice, so it took him longer.

"Brown fur!" he thought. "Victorious has brown fur, and some of it is tan as well." Up until now the only colors in the forest had been shades of yellow, but now he could see browns as well. And then he remembered the sodaberries - they had definitely been purple. He still had their stains on his shirt. Looking down, Niles could see the distinct purple tinge of the berry spots on his sleeves.

"Frederick!" Niles shouted, much too loud for the comforting silence of the Glen. "Victorious has _brown_ fur." The startled ferret, awakened from a dream in which the world was filled with Gather bushes, stared up at him sleepily, hardly knowing what to say.

"Yes," he answered finally. "That's true."

But Niles went on excitedly. "And the sodaberries were purple. See, I still have the stains here." He proudly exhibited his shirtsleeve to Frederick and waited expectantly for a response.

The ferret was bewildered. All he could think of to say was "Well, be more careful the next time you eat berries."

"He is seeing more colors now, Frederick," called Henrietta, watching from her perch. Turning her wise face towards Niles, she continued: "As you journey through the Forest, you grow."

Niles looked down at himself, but he didn't seem any taller.

"Not taller," hooted the owl. "You grow wiser. You learn things about yourself. You find strengths you didn't know you had. That's what your journey is all about."

Niles was glad someone had finally told him how this "journey" worked. It was true that he had learned about himself and about other people as well. He had learned to look at things from their viewpoint, and to care about their feelings. What was even more important to him, he had bested Calamidrake several times, and that was something he had never been able to do before.

Still, he was uneasy, and a persistent sinking feeling hidden vaguely in a small corner of his mind said that the Dragon wasn't finished with him. In this he was, unfortunately, very, very right.

He was about to ask Henrietta another question, but the owl answered before he had a chance. "As you grow, the Forest lets you see more and more colors. And other things change as well. What more have you noticed?"

Niles thought about it, but Frederick, recovered from his confusion, interrupted. Stretching his front paws over the log where he had been dozing, and looking first one way and then the other to make sure everyone was listening, he quipped "Well, he hasn't gotten any neater. Just look at his shirt. And his pants too."

"Hush," replied Henrietta. "Let him think."

Frederick didn't exactly hush, but he did chortle a little more softly. Finally, Niles suggested hesitantly that "it seemed to be a little easier walking along the path, and the path might be a little bit straighter."

"Good!" hooted the owl. "Gaining strength is good, but realizing that you are growing is just as important. What else?"

"Well," responded Niles, warmed by the praise, "the Sun shines more often, and the trees don't block out as much of the sky. I wonder if there will be more stars in the sky tonight."

"Oh, yes," grinned Henrietta, "there will be more."

"And," continued Niles, getting more and more enthusiastic, "I smell more things. At first, I could only smell the honeysuckle, but now I can tell that there are different odors in the forest." He took a deep breath through his nose. "Oak," he said, "I smell oak. And pine. I smell the moist air from the river, and something else ..." He paused to sniff again a few times, a puzzled look on his face. "I don't know what it is, but is sweet and a little like grapes and a little like oranges ..."

"It's your shirt," whooped Frederick, almost falling over backwards laughing. "Yes, yes, yes! Sodaberry stains on your shirt. That's what they smell like."

Niles smelled the stains on his sleeve. Sure enough, that was the puzzling aroma. He joined the others in a good laugh. When they had gotten as much merriment as they could out of Niles and his shirt, everyone began to relax and enjoy the sights, sounds, and smells of the Glen of Discovery.

Henrietta closed her eyes and seemed to fall asleep. Niles wondered why she didn't fall off of her perch, but apparently owls could sleep standing up. Victorious brushed off a few specks of dust on Morning Gloria's leaves and sat back against a tree. What he was thinking,

Niles couldn't tell. Frederick stretched his back against the tree trunk and contentedly used the rough bark to scratch himself. Niles was very relaxed and was starting to think. And that was how the trouble began.

Niles thought about home and about his parents. He remembered how he had felt earlier that day. He had been sad. His parents must be missing him and wondering where he was. They wouldn't know if he was even alive and they would be terribly worried. As Niles got sadder and sadder, his face fell and a tear crept out of the corner of his eye and ran part of the way down his cheek.

Then suddenly, "POP!" there was a sound like a small explosion and Calamidrake was back.

Niles was startled and more than a little concerned. This wasn't how the Dragon usually appeared. Most of the time, it came into Niles' mind slowly, gradually getting bigger and changing from blue to orange or even red. But this time it was just there, all at once, filling Niles' thoughts and looking very commanding. It was already at least half red and steam came out of both nostrils in a steady flow.

"Just what I expected," said the Dragon, smugly. "You say you feel badly for your parents, but then you forget them for the whole day. I'm surprised you remembered about them at all. Maybe with your friends asleep and nothing else to do you finally found some time. Even I treated my mother better than you do. Of course, I ate my father, and that wasn't so nice, but I was always good to my mother. Good for a Dragon, that is."

You see, the Ugly-Thoughts Dragon never actually lied. It told a kind of truth, distorted like what you see through splashing water, but still sort of true. This was part of its strength. If the Dragon lied, Niles would have caught him in the lies and never listened to him again. But by saying things that were partly true and not exactly false, it kept Niles believing. That was what it was doing now. When the Dragon said he was good to his mother, he had to go on and say "Good for a Dragon, that is," in order to make it a little bit true.

Niles was confused by his sad feelings and by Calamidrake just "popping" into his head. He believed the things the Dragon was saying. They had a ring of truth to them, but there was also something wrong. Unfortunately, Niles couldn't tell just what the flaw was.

A blast of steam from Calamidrake seared Niles' neck. The evil beast was laughing as hard as it could, pausing just long enough once in a while to shoot out another hot jet of vapor. "Maybe it's time you did something about these feelings of yours. If you really have them." The Dragon was in rare form. "All you have to do is say 'I quit' three times and this unpleasant Forest will disappear. You'll be home with your mother and father. That's what you want, isn't it?"

Niles couldn't deny that he missed home desperately. He shoved his hand in his pocket and clasped his lucky stone, looking for the strength to resist the Dragon. It helped for a moment. The spell of Calamidrake's words faded slightly, and Niles began to see that quitting now was what the Dragon wanted, and not what he wanted.

But lucky stones have only so much power and, as the moments passed, it faded and then was gone entirely. Niles still could feel the stone clenched in his fist, but it was hard and cold. The lucky stone had done what it could by bringing back images of happy moments in the past, but now Niles had to deal with the present.

Niles had never seen Calamidrake so completely red. There was not a trace of blue, green, yellow or orange anywhere on its scale-covered body. Only its head remained a very dark green. Nor had he ever seen it so large and powerful. Almost without willing it, Niles' lips opened and he whispered "I quit."

"Go on," urged the Dragon, "say it twice more and this will all be over. Go on! Go on! Say it!"

Calamidrake now filled almost all Niles' mind, but there was still a tiny corner that was his own. In that small remaining sanctuary, he heard a voice. "There is no danger in this Forest," the voice whispered, "except what you bring here yourself." It sounded like the Slow River, Itasara. "And there is nothing that you brought that you cannot overcome. We have all been helping you, but now you need to try to help yourself."

A surge of strength filled Niles. Calamidrake recoiled as if hit by a blow. He shrank to half his size (still enormous) and for a few moments ceased to blow scalding steam through his nostrils. Niles knew he had a chance and he fought with all of his remaining strength. "Go away, go away!" he shouted at the top of his voice, shutting his eyes as hard as he could and concentrating deeply and profoundly on making the Dragon disappear.

But the Dragon was even now recovering his strength. Its legs had faded to yellow, and there was even a touch of green around its toes, but it was no longer falling backwards. "No!" it roared, "that won't work this time. You made me pop out before by thinking about other things. That just makes me go away for a little while. Sooner or later you have to face me. You were sad about your parents. That's why I came. You never fixed that. You just made me pop out for a little while. Now I'm back. Now you have to deal with your feelings and with me. There is no escape. Say 'I quit'. Say it!"

And Niles did say it. "I quit," he said, much stronger than the last time.

"Once more," urged the Dragon. "Once more!"

Understanding flooded over Niles. This time the Dragon had told the exact truth. He had not dealt with his feelings of sadness about missing his parents. He had been distracted by Victorious and by the other wonderful happenings of the day. But these feelings didn't die, they just were hidden for a time. He did have to deal with them.

The Dragon's truthfulness made his command to quit much harder to resist. Still, there was a spark deep within Niles' brain that said to him "Quitting is not the way to deal with this problem. There are better ways. Get rid of the Dragon and then find the right path. _That's_ what this journey is all about."

The pull of the Dragon might still have gotten Niles. He might have said that third "I quit." The journey might have ended. Niles would then have been back home, but Calamidrake would have won. It would still be in control, and who knows when, if ever, Niles would get a chance for another journey.

Just then something happened. Niles heard a song. He looked around, but Frederick, Henrietta, Victorious, and Morning Gloria were silent and motionless, as if in a trance. They definitely weren't singing.

Then Niles realized that the song was inside his own head. He recognized it as one that his parents used to sing to him whenever he was sad, scared, confused, or sometimes even when he was just happy. He remembered the song from a time before Calamidrake had come into his world. There had been no place for the Dragon then, because Niles' world had been filled with songs.

He began to hum the song softly, a few notes at a time, and then more loudly. Soon Niles started singing out loud. It felt good to know he had a song to sing. Victorious and Frederick awoke from their silence and joined in.

Calamidrake wasn't singing. In fact, he looked terribly upset, as if he had almost had what he wanted most in all the world, and then it had been taken way. Suddenly, the spell of the Dragon was broken. With a mournful shriek, Calamidrake spun around and around and around and around getting smaller all the while, like a balloon when someone lets the air out of it. And then it was gone.

Niles slumped to the ground, exhausted. He had escaped, but just by an inch. Without the song ... he didn't want to think about what would have happened without the song. Where had it come from? "Itasara!" he thought to himself. "It must have been Itasara who rescued me, in the end."

"Yes," came the river's voice, "I helped by freeing the song in your memory. But it was your song all along. I helped a very little bit. Next time you will do it on your own."

"No," wailed Niles, aloud this time. "I can't. I can't." But Itasara didn't answer. The leaves of the nearby trees rustled in the gentle breeze. "I can't," he whispered one more time. But he thought that maybe he could.

Chapter 15 - To Sleep, Perchance to Dream

The forest floor felt cool and damp beneath Niles, as he lay there thinking about the events of the past hour. It was very disturbing, even though in the end everything had worked out well.

One thing in particular kept bothering Niles. "Next time you will do it on your own," Itasara had said. Having to handle the Dragon himself was bad enough, but now it was the "next time" that was making Niles nervous. "Would these encounters with Calamidrake never end?" he asked himself. "Wasn't this journey supposed to be to get rid of that burden forever?"

It seemed to Niles that nothing was being accomplished. True, he had discovered strengths in himself. True, he had been able to make Calamidrake turn and flee, and more than once. And, of course, he had made wonderful friends. But for this journey to succeed, did not the Dragon have to be banished forever? Niles felt no nearer to that goal than the day he had first set foot in the Endless Forest.

Just then Niles heard a tiny popping sound a few feet behind him. "Oh, no," he thought, "not the Dragon popping in again! Not so soon!" But, as you have surely guessed, it wasn't Calamidrake at all. Niles found that out when he turned his head and saw Frederick contently lying next to him on his back. His rear paws were stretched out pointing towards the river, and his front paws were folded over his chest. As Niles watched, the ferret blew a tiny bubble.

"Pop" went the bubble softly, as Frederick sucked it back into his mouth and began chewing again. Presently he saw Niles watching him chew, so he decided to blow a really big bubble. As the bubble began to grow and grow and grow, Frederick puffed into it harder and harder and harder, until, instead of popping, the entire blob exploded out of his mouth, went straight up into the air, came right back down and hit the surprised ferret squarely in the nose.

The noise of Frederick's effort had broken the near silence on the Forest floor, and everyone was looking at him. Even Morning Gloria turned her petals his way. Now they all broke out with a tremendous roar. Henrietta hooted so loudly that she lost hold of her branch with one foot and ended up swinging head down until she could regain her balance.

Niles looked at his first Forest friend anxiously, but Frederick was laughing as hard as anyone. They were all laughing together. They were laughing _with_ Frederick, not _at_ him.

At that moment, Niles understood something about himself. Many times his friends had laughed at things he did, and usually Niles would react with anger, with Calamidrake urging him on. And now Niles realized that he could have laughed along with them instead. It seems so obvious, but he had never thought of it before. So Niles grinned, and then he snickered, and then he burst out with as loud a laugh as any of his friends.

Frederick had regained his composure enough to retrieve his wad of beeswax - for that is what it was, a gift from Victorious. It wasn't nearly as good as chewing gum, and it was only with the greatest effort that Frederick could blow bubbles with it, but chewing gum was not to be found in the Endless Forest, so the ferret made do with what he could get.

Niles was actually the first to speak. "When I heard the 'pop'," he said, "I was afraid Calamidrake had come back. After all, I still haven't dealt with my sadness about missing my parents and being worried about them."

"It's okay to miss your folks," said Victorious soothingly. "We all do sometimes."

"Being a little sad isn't so bad," chimed in Henrietta. "It goes away eventually, especially when you sing happy songs. Do you know any good ones, Niles?"

"Oh, yes," answered Niles quickly. "I used one to chase away the Dragon a little while ago. It goes like this," and he began to hum the tune.

"We know it," hooted the owl. "You sang it very loudly when you were chasing the Dragon. It's a great song." And with that, all of the friends began singing it together. It went something like this:

Hush-a-bye, don't you cry.

Go to sleep my little ba-by.
When you wake, you will see
All the pretty little hor-sees.
Dapples and grays, pintos and bays -
All the pretty little hor-sees.

Singing this song made everyone feel joyful.

Niles learned that feelings are okay, that they are temporary, and that they are an important part of being a person. And as they sang Niles' song, he started feeling better - much better.

The Glen of Discovery had been a wonderful place to spend the afternoon, but evening was creeping through the treetops, and the shadows were growing longer and longer in the sweet-smelling forest air. They ate a quick dinner of jelly sandwiches (the peanut butter had run out), honey, nuts, and berries, and washed it all down with cool river water, courtesy of Itasara. Now it was time to continue the journey.

Niles noticed that the path was less curvy, and he was able to go further that day than the first. Still, he was getting tired. Frederick, Henrietta, and Victorious never complained; they just walked alongside. They did not speak much but Niles felt his friends' presence with every step. He enjoyed feeling protected, accepted, and happy. Funny, he had never thought in terms of feelings before. But then again, he had never had such adventures before!

Niles was very tired and ready to drop from exhaustion, but his bed was nowhere to be seen. Then he remembered what Roger had said to him. "Take one more step," his friend had told him. "One more step," Niles thought, "or better yet, two more steps."

With the last of his strength, Niles took two more steps, and there it was -- his comfortable, safe bed lying just to the side of the path under the sheltering branches of an old oak tree.

Niles didn't even take off his clothes. Kicking off his shoes, he practically jumped into bed. Frederick curled up right at his feet, and Henrietta perched on the headboard, just inches from his right ear. Victorious just plumped down beside him and pulled the cover over him. Actually, it didn't completely cover the bear. In fact, it didn't even completely cover his belly, because Victorious was a _very_ big bear.

"Strange," Niles thought, "just last week he had told his mother that he was outgrowing his bed, but now all of them fit comfortably with room to spare. He did not mind sharing his space with his friends, although to tell the complete truth, he was a little anxious about what might happen if Victorious rolled over in his sleep.

His friends had fallen asleep, except for Frederick who was washing his paws with his tongue. Niles was getting very drowsy. As he lay there, Niles thought of his day and all his adventures. He had overcome most of his fears the first day, so now the journey was becoming an exciting adventure. There were new sights, more colors, sounds, and smells all around him. He had managed to fend off Calamidrake (though it had been a close call), and he had taken *two* additional steps when he was truly exhausted. It had been a good day; not an easy day, but a good day. He began to look forward to the third day of his journey.

"Do you ever dream?" he asked Frederick softly.

"Sure," answered the ferret.

"About what?"

Frederick was silent for a while and Niles was beginning to think he hadn't heard or perhaps had fallen asleep. But eventually his friend answered, speaking in a very soft voice and, it seemed to Niles, a little sadly. "I dream of a home" was all he said.

"Home?" Niles had never thought about the ferret having a home. "Where is your home, anyway? Do you have a wife and children?"

That seemed to amuse Frederick. "No, no, no," he chuckled, "no wife, no children. I'm not old enough for that yet!" He curled himself up a little more tightly and snuggled deeper into the covers. "I don't have a home either. Oh, the Endless Forest is my home. All of it. A wonderful place to live. So many interesting people and animals. New journeys and adventures every week. Still, sometimes I think I would like a home. A little house with flowers growing around it. A big wooden door and big windows all around. A cheerful room with a sofa and a fireplace. And stairs leading up to a bedroom all my own."

Niles was very sleepy now. "That sounds a lot like my home," he mumbled, as he tucked his chin under the blanket and his own dream world surrounded him.

"I know," the ferret said, and then he, too, fell asleep.

Chapter 16 - A Meeting of the Minds (Almost)

Niles opened one eye. It wouldn't have done him any good to open the other eye because it was covered by his blanket. Yes, it was morning. The birds were chirping, the tree branches were swaying in the light gentle breeze, and there was a soft light filtering through the foliage and making its way here and there to the forest floor.

It was Niles' third day in the Forest. Things were going well, he told himself. On the first day he had mostly gotten rid of fear and on the second day he had gained courage. He felt stronger. He had learned to feel the pain of another, and he had learned that feelings, even including pain, were temporary. He had faced Sir Draconis of the Ugly-Thoughts and had won, with a little help from his friends. He would get by.

Niles noticed that the less happy experiences faded away into deep memory, memories such as how he had accidentally hurt Victorious and how Calamidrake had almost gotten him to say "I quit" three times; these memories did not cause him to shudder and feel badly; they seemed to have little power over him. They were just there, stored away in a memory chest, perhaps recalled at times if needed, but just there. He had mastered the feelings that went with the memories and moved on.

"This is great!" he thought to himself. "This is the way to wake up in the morning, learning from experiences, remembering the good times and looking forward to the new day." He was congratulating himself on this discovery when he opened both eyes wide and found that he had been looking directly at Morning Gloria.

How she had changed! In the slanting rays of the cool morning Sun, Morning Gloria's flowers were wide open. Stem after stem was covered in beautiful blue blooms with pure white centers. The dark green leaves were a perfect background to the flowers, each one perfect and turned towards the Sun.

Everyone seemed to be drawing strength from Morning Gloria. Victorious lay on his side next to Morning Gloria's pot and watched her fondly. Frederick paced slowly around her, examining the flower from every direction, and Henrietta swooped down low over her from time to time, fanning the stems and flowers with the draft from her powerful wings.

Of course, Niles had also been affected by the plant. He suddenly understood. "So," he said to Morning Gloria, "you gave me all of those happy thoughts when I woke up."

The answer came from over his head, where Henrietta was slowly circling, avoiding tree branches most cleverly and dipping low when she approached Niles. "Not really. Morning Gloria brings hope. You did the rest yourself."

"Hope?" questioned Niles.

"Surely you know what hope is," Frederick chided.

"Hope is morning, and morning is hope."

Niles looked around in surprise. "Who was that?" he asked.

Once again Henrietta flew close to Niles and was the one to answer. "That was Itasara. It's hard to tell what she means sometimes."

"It's hard to tell what Itasara means _all_ of the time," thought Niles. The river chuckled causing gentle ripples in its flow.

"Hope is what you felt this morning," Itasara said, her voice slowly fading away into the depths of his mind. Niles strained to hear more but the presence of the river was gone for now. It didn't matter; he didn't need the river to finish the thought. Niles understood. He actually understood something Itasara had said! With a fond glance at Morning Gloria, he announced "Of course, I know what hope is!"

Victorious nodded his head towards Niles, then turned and picked up Morning Gloria. After making sure she was in a sunny spot, the bear went off in search of breakfast. Victorious had appointed himself chef and took his job seriously. Niles had never imagined that the Forest could provide such delicious foods. There was always honey and many kinds of nuts and berries.

While Victorious foraged, Niles had time to look around. He could see much more clearly today than even yesterday. There were more colors, especially greens and blues in a fantastic number of shades and mixtures. All around him were colorful flowers. There were daisies with white petals and black centers, and some with yellow petals and white centers, and a few with pale blue petals and dark blue centers. All had light green leaves that reminded Niles of the ferns that grew along the bank of the stream near his home.

There were flowers whose names Niles didn't know, some with lots of dark shiny leaves and some with a few gigantic leaves with bright green surfaces laced with darker lines. A plant with particularly dark and shiny leaves growing in groups of three attracted Niles' attention, and he walked over to look at it more closely.

"Don't touch," came Frederick's voice, as the ferret scurried over beside him. "That's poison I.V. I think it has something that gets into your blood and makes you itch."

Niles drew back as if he had touched a hot pan. Fortunately, he had only looked at the plant. "I didn't think there was anything in the forest that was dangerous," he said imploringly.

"Dangerous? Dangerous, yes," Frederick answered. "The Forest has many things that are dangerous if you are not careful."

"Like what?" Niles wanted to know, with his eyes open wide and his ears at attention.

Frederick's thoughts seemed to be in another world. "Yes, dangerous things," was all he said. Niles wondered what he meant. Forest creatures all seemed to have secrets. He eyed the ferret warily, but quickly reminded himself that Frederick was his friend.

Just then Victorious returned humming a tune Niles had never heard before. His arms were full of jars, packages, and a huge picnic basket. Niles could smell the honey and some kind of berry. There were also nuts, of course, and small tomatoes, medium-size carrots, and a very, very, very large watermelon. Except for the carrots, this was exactly Niles' kind of breakfast!

As soon as Victorious had laid everything out on a grassy area next to the path (and that was very soon indeed), Niles, Frederick, Henrietta and two or three squirrels that happened to be passing by sat down enthusiastically to the fine meal.

How they all enjoyed it! Niles was delighted with the tastes and smells of the food. He started telling stories, about his school and his friends in his world, and the various adventures he had had before entering the Endless Forest.

Everyone was listening closely to his tales; even Morning Gloria turned her leaves his way. Niles never knew he was such a good storyteller. It felt good to have someone listen. It felt good to make others laugh rather than watch them frown.

And so, he talked on and on and on, about Ms. Stern and Ms. Knowall, his teachers, and Ms. Greenstem and her garden (or what was left of it), and mostly about his good friend Roger and the fun they had together. This was going to be a great day! Or so Niles thought.

Breakfast was soon finished. Quickly, the companions washed in a small brook that fed into the Slow River, and then began walking briskly along the forest path. It led them slowly uphill. Still Niles talked on. If his friends were getting tired of his stories, they gave no indication of it.

I won't bother you with the stories right now, because, for one thing, they would make this book too long. And besides, something interesting is about to happen and you would probably like to get to that part as soon as possible.

In any case, as Niles was walking and talking and taking and walking while enjoying the colors, he stumbled into a big rock. That's what happens when you aren't watching where you are going. This time, Niles stubbed his big toe and yelled out in irritation. He had been having such a good time that he hadn't noticed the big rock in the middle of the road, and he did not react quickly enough when Henrietta called out to warn him.

When Niles hit his foot on the rock, he yelled so loudly that he barely heard the big rock yell out in pain at the same time.

"A talking giant rock?" thought Niles through his pain. "What next?" At most times, encountering a talking rock would fascinate Niles, just as it would surely get your attention. Right now he was irritated with himself for hurting his toe, and this began to turn into anger. Besides feeling his pain, Niles did not like hurting anything, not even a giant rock. When the rock yelled out in pain, Niles became even more upset.

He noticed his friend, Frederick, jump away from him, and Victorious hold Morning Gloria protectively. They could see that he was losing control. Niles was familiar with these responses; his friends outside of the forest did it all the time. Now, however, it only further annoyed him. "I would never hurt my friends!" he thought. "Not on purpose, anyway."

I'm sure you have guessed what was coming next - the dreaded hiss. Niles had opened the door for Calamidrake. "You clumsy wimp," it began.

Niles looked at his friends' anxious faces and at Morning Gloria, and he felt their strength. He remembered the song his parents used to sing to him when he was little. "Hush-a-bye, don't you cry ..." It reminded him of his parents and the good times singing that he and his friends Frederick and Victorious had the day before. Immediately Niles felt powerful.

Calamidrake sensed the turn of events and was not pleased. Oh, no, not pleased at all, not one bit. Presently Niles was shouting at him: "I was not watching where I was going. That does not make me a clumsy wimp. I made a mistake, that's all. I'm not a bad person and I'm _not_ going to hurt my friends." Apparently, it worked because the Dragon decided not to make a stand this time. Quickly, he curled himself up in his tail and looked very small and far away. Niles just forgot about him.

He apologized to Frederick, Victorious, and Morning Gloria for upsetting them with his anger. Suddenly he heard a voice say: "You should be apologizing to me." It came from the direction of the giant rock on which he had stubbed his toe, so Niles assumed it was a talking rock. "Sorry I hurt you, big rock," he said in his friendliest tone.

"Not the rock. Me!" retorted the brightest green iguana he had ever seen. It had been sunning itself on the rock all along, and Niles had accidentally pinched its tail. The iguana looked down at Niles and his friends. Victorious and Henrietta immediately recognized her. "This is Claracuca, a good friend of ours," said the owl.

"What kind of a name is Claracuca?" Niles said to himself.

"A name from the earth. A name children love to say," answered the iguana.

"Oh no, another mind-reading creature!" thought Niles.

Hearing the commotion, Frederick had scampered over. When he saw what had happened, he explained to Niles that Claracuca loved the Sun, and would sit on a big rock where it is usually warm.

Niles was fascinated by Claracuca. He had seen an iguana once before when his friend Jimmy had brought his pet to school. Claracuca was much larger though; in fact, she was nearly as long as Niles was tall. She looked like most lizards, which is not surprising since iguanas are in the lizard family. In a way, Claracuca reminded Niles of Calamidrake, but he dismissed that thought from his mind as soon as it entered. Not quite quickly enough however.

Claracuca looked at Niles with lazy eyes, very slowly moving her head from side to side. "So, he caught up with you, I see," she said, referring, of course, to the Dragon.

"You know too?"

"Who doesn't?" answered Claracuca lazily, while making funny motions with her very pink tongue.

That silenced Niles for a moment, and his friends took advantage of the pause to climb up on the rock and join Claracuca in the sunshine. Niles noticed that Claracuca moved slowly and deliberately. It was like she thought about each movement before making it. That seemed to make sense, but Niles wondered if the iguana could ever move quickly. She would never be good at those television game shows - the ones where you had to be the first to push a button to answer a question. He laughed at the image of Claracuca being the first to push a button.

"You'd be surprised at what we can do when we need to do it," remarked Claracuca.

"Mind readers! These forest creatures must all be mind readers," thought Niles. He was a little bit irritated. These were all his friends, but he would have liked to have a few private thoughts. At least he hoped they were his friends, because if they weren't ...

In truth, Niles was beginning to get a little bit nervous. Frederick, Victorious, Henrietta, and now Claracuca all seemed to know each other very well. They were each different, of course, but there was a sameness about them that didn't seem quite normal. Were they really his friends?

Niles dismissed these thoughts from his mind, but he did decide to try an experiment. He shut his eyes and mouth and thought very, very hard: "If you hear what I'm thinking, tell me your favorite color."

In less time than it takes to think of an answer, Niles got his responses.

"Brown," Frederick piped up.

"Black," hooted Henrietta. "Is that a color?" asked Frederick. "Of course, it is," answered the owl.

"Gold, the color of honey," said Victorious, "and blue like Morning Gloria." He gazed fondly at the potted plant. "No fair," chimed in Frederick, "that's two colors."

"Green, of course". That was from Claracuca. "Cool rain" responded Morning Gloria. "I know that's not a color," complained Frederick.

Several other voices answered, too, saying "Grey" (possibly Itasara), "Red" (it could have been the Ugly-Thoughts Dragon), "White" and "Pink". Niles had no idea who gave the last two answers.

It was true. Niles' experiment had revealed that these forest creatures could read minds. That was clear enough, but there was also a thought in the back of Niles' brain that couldn't quite break free. There was something more to this mind-reading business, he realized. But what? It seemed to Niles that he would have to find out if he was to successfully complete this journey.

"I think he's figured it out," said Henrietta.

Niles interrupted abruptly. "Figured what out?" There was silence for a minute. "What?" Niles repeated.

"No, he doesn't quite have it yet," was all the answer he got. That was Itasara. Niles had understood what she meant once today (about "hope") but now things were back to normal - he had no idea what the river was talking about.

Chapter 17 - The Road Goes Ever On

Now that Claracuca had decided to join his group of friends, Niles had to admit that he was concerned that the iguana would slow them down. In fact, when he and Frederick had walked twenty or thirty steps down the path, Claracuca was still sunning herself on her rock.

Slowly, the iguana turned her beautiful bright green head away from the Sun and looked at Niles. Niles looked back over his shoulder, and was about to say something like "Hurry up, if you can," but he never got the chance. When Claracuca moved, she really moved. Sliding gracefully off the rock, she got her feet under her and, in the blink of an eye, had caught up with them.

"Wow!" exclaimed Niles. "You are _really_ fast!"

"Why does that surprise you?" asked Claracuca.

Niles was a little bit embarrassed but decided he could say just what he felt, so long as he was careful to do it nicely and politely. "Well, you seemed to do everything so carefully that I thought ..."

Claracuca finished the sentence for him. "You thought I was slow."

Niles hung his head. He remembered how he had accidentally pinched Claracuca's tail, and he now knew that words could also hurt. "I guess so" was all he said, in a small voice.

Claracuca faced Niles directly. She would have put her hands on her hips, in order to look irritated, only she didn't have any hips. Frederick, Henrietta, and Victorious were watching the scene with barely-concealed merriment. Niles wasn't at all amused.

Frederick broke out laughing first. In an instant, he was joined by all of the others, and in two instants, Niles realized that Claracuca wasn't angry at all.

"Claracuca loves to pull that stunt," explained Henrietta between hoots.

"It's a good joke," said Niles. "It certainly had me fooled."

"Things are not always what they seem," Claracuca responded.

"In this Forest, things are *never* what they seem," answered Niles. Then he wondered whether that included friends.

Niles had little time to wonder, however, as the party quickly resumed their trip down the path, now nearly straight and flat. The trees no longer closed in so tightly. There were grassy green meadows where fields of yellow daisies grew, and, now and then, a small brook winding its way slowly towards a meeting with a greater body of water.

The colors of the flowers, grasses, and trees brightened as the Sun broke through. Every shade of yellow, blue, green, brown, and purple found its place in a flower petal or the bark of a tree or the wings of a butterfly. "That's strange," thought Niles, "there are no reds or oranges. I wonder if that's because those are the Dragon's mean colors."

Niles' thoughts wandered with him through the forest, now focusing on the smells of the pine trees and now on the feel of the path under his feet, which was steadily growing more stony. Presently, they came to a larger creek, almost a river in its own right. It was too wide to jump over and flowed so swiftly that even Victorious eyed it skeptically.

"How do we get across this?" asked Niles to no one in particular.

Frederick had no idea. Henrietta had no problem (she could fly over it.) Victorious had no hands -- no hands free, that is, since he was carrying Morning Gloria in one and the basket with the remains of breakfast in the other. Claracuca dipped one foot into the water and declared that she had no thought of going into water that cold!

Now the path at this point split into two. One part went to the creek and the other bent left along its bank and ran off into the distance. "What's that way?" asked Niles, pointing to the latter route.

"Oh, that's the Left Banke," answered Victorious. "And this creek is called the Sane. You don't want to fall into it, because then you would be 'In Sane'." He laughed to himself.

"What's he talking about?" Niles asked Claracuca.

"Paris," answered the iguana.

"Paris? What does this have to do with Paris?"

"Don't mind her," interrupted Frederick, "she dipped her foot in the river, so she's a little bit In Sane. It will go away soon."

Niles was getting slightly annoyed. "Well does anyone know where this path goes?"

"I know," said Henrietta. It follows the creek which gets wider and wider. After a while it flows into The Bay."

"Isn't a bay very large?" asked Niles dubiously. "How could we ever cross it?"

"Cross the bay? No, we can't cross the bay. No way." Frederick began to chant "No way to cross the bay ... no, no. No way to cross the bay ... ho ho." He seemed very pleased with himself. Niles ignored him; obviously the ferret was not going to be much help.

"Before we get to The Bay," Henrietta continued, raising her voice to be heard over Frederick's chanting, "there is a bridge. We can cross there."

"Ok, that sounds good. We'll go that way." Niles was starting to make the decisions for the travelers.

Claracuca looked doubtful. Frederick stopped chanting. He looked at Victorious and said: "that's the Bridge of Passage." He seemed troubled. Victorious had a worried look.

Henrietta alone seemed positive. "True, but he must go that way sooner or later. That is, if he wants to complete his journey." She turned to Niles. "Do you?" she asked.

"Of course," he answered quickly. "But what's wrong with the Bridge of Passage? Is it dangerous?"

"Oh, the Bridge is sturdy enough," responded Henrietta. "But it usually is guarded. I can tell you no more so don't ask," she went on when she noticed that Niles was about to voice another question.

Niles closed his mouth and didn't say anything. He would have liked to ask a great number of questions, such as "Guarded by whom?" and "Is there another way?" but it was clear that his friends were not going to tell him any more. Besides, since no one was willing to cross the Sane, they had to take the path along the Left Banke. Niles shouldered his backpack, now much lighter but still containing many of his favorite things, and began following the path as it wound along the creek bank.

At first, the Left Banke was open, with only a few trees near by. The creek, now grown to a river, was easily visible on their right, and flowers grew next to the path. But the path itself was stony, and shortly it because downright rocky. Some of the rocks were so large that the party had to squeeze by them or even walk off of the path. This they didn't like to do, because swamps came up to the edges of the path in places, often hidden by tall grass. Only the path seemed completely safe and wholesome.

They stopped for lunch, which was mainly the leftovers from breakfast and drank cold water from the river. It was okay to drink from the river now, because the Sane had joined with other streams, creeks and small rivers. Now it was called the Lorenzo and was no longer dangerous.

So far, the walk had been uneventful. Frederick and Henrietta had been out hunting since mice were abundant along the river. Victorious was absorbed in adding a few pinches of new dirt to Morning Gloria's pot and pressing them down carefully around her roots. Claracuca was strutting along in front, her quick little pink tongue sampling the aromas of the moist river air. Occasionally she snagged a tasty bug.

The forest had come back towards the path as the party entered a small valley. On both sides, hills rose gently, cupping the path in their embrace and leading it onwards into deepening stands of dark pine and oak trees with bent branches.

As the day wore on, the hills on either side of the path got higher and squeezed in closer to the travelers. They were not threatening, and Niles wasn't afraid; well, not exactly. He felt a little, shall we say, uncomfortable.

Occasionally, when a large rock appeared in their path, they had to scramble over it because there wasn't enough room at the sides of the path to go around.

It was still early in the afternoon, but Niles was getting tired. The weather was warm and climbing rocks took a lot of effort. Periodically the Sun disappeared behind an outcropping of rock and the path became gray and gloomy. Niles began to wonder if they had gone the wrong way after all. He began looking for side paths, but there were none to be found.

Just when he thought that he would have to stop and rest, the party came upon the biggest rock Niles had ever seen. It completely blocked their path. The valley had become more like a canyon, and the rock reached from wall to wall. There might have been a tiny crawling space beneath the rock, but that would do them little good.

Niles was discouraged. "I give up" he said. Calamidrake stirred. "You have to say 'I quit'," it reminded Niles.

"Forget it!" Niles snapped at the Dragon.

"I will," it said, curling back into its tail. "But you won't."

Chapter 18 - Rock Me Gently

A good day had suddenly turned very bad. Niles was facing a huge rock, as big as a wall (you might even call it a boulder) and he could find no way past it. He was very tired, and he was hungry. Victorious had run out of food and didn't seem inclined to search for any more.

Niles was frustrated. He was starting to become _very_ frustrated. And when that happened, he usually began to get angry.

Sure enough, he _was_ beginning to get angry. By now, Niles knew that if he allowed his anger to grow, he would never come up with a solution to his problem. Worse, he would be opening the door for Calamidrake. He thought again, "What can I do?" Then he listened carefully, hoping that one of his friends, or maybe even Itasara, would read his thoughts and give him the answer.

No one did.

Looking around, Niles saw that his friends were as puzzled as he. Victorious sat on the ground, holding Morning Gloria in one paw and scratching his head with the other. Frederick paced back and forth, every now and then turning his head to glare at the rock. Claracuca had gone into her slow-motion act and Henrietta appeared to be sleeping standing up.

Niles had grown used to his friends' guidance, but this time it was clearly up to him. "That's not fair," he thought, "it's their Forest, not mine!" Calamidrake uncurled its tail and sent out an exploratory wisp of steam from its left nostril.

"Oops," Niles said to himself, "I'd better stop thinking negative thoughts." He forced himself to think only positive things about his friends, remembering all the times they had helped and comforted him. "After all, it is _my_ journey," he explained to himself. "I've been growing stronger and learning new things, so I can surely find a way around a boulder." The Dragon went back to sleep, but Niles noticed that it kept one eye open just a little bit.

Niles sat down in the middle of the path facing the boulder and tried to think of a way to get past it. He noticed that there was a small opening at ground level to his left, where the bottom of the rock didn't quite reach to the canyon wall. "Maybe I can crawl under it," he thought to himself.

Just at that moment, Frederick stopped his pacing and headed for that very opening. He tried to squeeze through it, but it was too small even for the ferret. Obviously, Niles would never be able to get through, to say nothing of Victorious!

"I wonder if we could dig around the hole to make it bigger," he said to himself. Instantly, Frederick started to scuff at the earth with his paws, throwing dirt and small stones behind him. The ferret worked feverishly, but three minutes later the hole was only a tiny bit bigger than it had been before.

"That won't work," thought Niles. Frederick stopped digging.

Now you may have noticed something rather odd. Whenever Niles thought something, Frederick tried to do it. Do you think Niles noticed? Of course, he did. But he was too absorbed in trying to get past the boulder to figure out what it meant. It reminded him of this morning, when he had met Claracuca and had found out that all of his friends could read his mind. There had been a thought in the back of his head then, and it was there again.

"No time to worry about that now," he said to himself, turning back to the problem of the boulder.

"It looks pretty smooth," Niles observed, "but maybe I can climb it." This time it was Claracuca who responded. Quickly, the iguana walked over to the huge rock and started looking for a way up. When she got to the far right, where the rock touched the canyon wall, she found a small bush growing out of the side of the cliff. Jumping as high as she could, she reached the bush and pulled herself over it, finding a low-hanging tree branch to hold on to.

The tree branch was quite small and bent under her weight, but she kept clawing and scrapping, from one doubtful hold to another, until finally she passed the overhang of the boulder and, with one great leap, landed on the lessening slope near the top of the rock. She had made it, and since it was sunny and warm on top, Claracuca promptly stretched out and went to sleep.

Niles was not hopeful. "I could never climb like that, and I'm sure Victorious would just pull the bushes and small trees out by the roots if he tried. But maybe Claracuca could pull me up." He walked over to the rock himself, but it was obvious that Claracuca could never reach him. He wasn't nearly tall enough. "Maybe Victorious could reach".

Obediently, the bear walked over to the rock and reached his paw up towards the iguana. Claracuca wrapped her tail around a knob of the rock and leaned over as far as she could, stretching out her paw to the bear. They just missed! But Victorious wasn't giving up. Putting Morning Gloria down gently in a sheltered area at the base of the rock, he tried again, this time on tiptoes. It was just enough - Victorious gripped Claracuca's front paw and the courageous iguana tried to pull him up.

Now you are probably thinking that this is ridiculous. How could an iguana, even one that was three feet long, ever hope to pull a gigantic bear like Victorious up to the top of the boulder? It seems impossible, doesn't it?

Well, it was impossible. Although his friends tried valiantly, Niles could see that this was not going to work. Dejectedly, he turned his back and walked away. Victorious got down off his tiptoes, picked up Morning Gloria, and sat in the shade at the side of the canyon. Claracuca resumed sunning herself at the top of the rock. Niles was starting to get very frustrated.

"Maybe I should just turn back," he thought, looking behind him at the path running off into the distance. Calamidrake opened its eye a little wider. "That would be a good idea," it agreed, peering watchfully at Niles.

If there was one lesson Niles had definitely learned, it was that if the Dragon liked something, it was sure to be bad for Niles. Still, if he couldn't go forward, and if the walls of the canyon stopped him from going to the side, all that was left was to go back. "I wonder what would happen if I did?" he said to himself.

Calamidrake answered, fully awake by now. "Nothing. Nothing would happen. Nothing at all." It had uncurled its tail. Its nose and ears were beginning to turn yellow. But it wasn't steaming and it seemed to be trying to restrain itself. This was strange behavior for Calamidrake. Niles wondered what it meant.

The Dragon had said that nothing would happen if he turned back. Niles knew, somehow, that the Dragon couldn't directly lie to him. It never had, but it usually didn't tell him _all_ of the truth and it often said things that could have many meanings.

"What do you mean when you say 'nothing' will happen?" Niles asked. He was getting quite cautious around "Sir Draconis of the Ugly-Thoughts."

The Dragon seemed to be uncomfortable and didn't want to answer, but Niles just waited. Eventually it got angry (that was a new one!) and spat out its response.

"Nothing! That's what I mean - nothing! The journey will be over. You will go back home. And nothing will have changed. Nothing!" Then it grew wistful and finished in a much lower voice. "Everything will be just like it was before the journey began," he said quietly as he curled his lips slightly up.

Now Niles understood. Turning back was exactly like saying "I quit" three times. Everything he had gained in the Forest would be lost! Niles was _not_ going to make that choice. "No," he answered simply, more to himself than to the Dragon. "There must be a way."

But what way? Although Niles had turned Calamidrake away, he still didn't have a solution to his problem. And he still was frustrated, and hot, and tired, and hungry. "What way? I can't get under it, and I can't climb it. For that matter, I don't even know if it will do any good to get past the boulder. I wonder if there even _is_ a path beyond it."

Now it was Henrietta who responded to his thought. Flapping her wings twice, she took off from the canyon floor, flying away from the boulder. But that was just to gain height; when she was high enough above the ground, she turned back in a graceful tight circle, flew over their heads and landed on a tree top just beyond the great rock. "The path goes on," she hooted back at them. "It's a fine path here. As soon as it passes the boulder, the canyon walls drop back and the path is very wide. It goes on as far as I can see (which was quite far), and there are sodaberry bushes full of fruit and the largest walnut tree I've ever seen."

The owl was excited, and the promise of delicious fruit and nuts gave Niles new energy. "Okay, okay," he thought, "so I can't go under the boulder, and I can't climb it. Maybe I can just push it a little bit. If the path widens out, all I need to do is move it a foot or two."

Victorious was at his side before Niles even finished the thought. Together they bent down and put their shoulders against the rock. "When I count to three, push with all your might," Niles directed.

"Wait!" cried Victorious. He was still holding Morning Gloria. Quickly, the bear found a safe spot, well away from the boulder, and set down the flowerpot. Then he returned to Niles and the rock.

"One," began Niles. Victorious pressed hard against the rock and prepared for the great effort. "Two ... Three." They both pushed with every ounce of their strength. For long seconds nothing happened. They were both tiring but were unwilling to give up. "Once more" gasped Niles, and they both shoved with everything they had. But it wasn't enough. The boulder didn't budge. It was just too heavy to push out of the way.

Niles and Victorious collapsed on the ground next to the rock, breathing heavily and wiping the sweat out of their eyes. After a few moments, Victorious got up and walked over to where he had left Morning Gloria. Picking up his friend, he returned to Niles' side.

Niles was sitting with his back to the rock. He was discouraged to say the least. All that would come into his mind was: "I just can't figure out the answer to this problem." Now was when he needed hope the most, but Morning Gloria's flowers were all closed. Then he heard a soft voice in his mind: "Hope is inside you," it said.

"That has to be Morning Gloria," thought Niles. "And she's right! If I keep up hope and keep thinking, I'll be able to solve this puzzle."

Did you notice the change in the word Niles used to describe his predicament? First it was a "problem." Now it is only a "puzzle." As I'm sure you know, "problems" can be like mountains and can be very hard to overcome, if not impossible. "Puzzles" are more like hills; solving them can be a challenge but it's always possible and usually fun.

Of course, all of this does not move a rock and, particularly, not a huge rock like the one in Niles' path. But he _was_ thinking. I suppose it was to think better, or maybe it was to see the problem more clearly, but for whatever reason Niles decided to get up. He had been resting with his back to a smaller very brown rock, not even as tall as he was. As he arose, he braced himself by placing a hand near the top of the brown rock. Then he pushed himself up.

He almost fell on his face! As soon as Niles pushed against the brown rock, it had rolled over! "Of course," Niles shouted excitedly. "I know how to move the boulder. Come on Victorious." He ran over to the big boulder with Victorious (who this time had remembered to put Morning Gloria in a safe place) following close behind.

"Put your paws on the rock as high as you can reach," Niles instructed his friend. "Then push it upwards. Maybe we can make it roll over!" Victorious did as he was told. He could reach past the middle of the rock, although not all the way to the top. He braced his legs and gave the boulder a solid push. It turned a few inches.

But then it stopped and rolled right back where it had been.

Claracuca woke with a start. "What happened? What happened?" she asked excitedly.

Henrietta hooted. "Sorry," answered Niles, "we're trying to roll the rock out of the way. I forgot you were sleeping up there. Maybe you had better get down." Claracuca needed no further urging. She slithered to the far side of the rock. Niles and Victorious could hear her as she slid down its side and jumped onto the path.

"Try again," Niles told the bear.

Victorious tried again, and once more the rock rolled a few inches and then settled back to its original position.

Niles rubbed his chin. "It's sticking on something," he suggested, "or perhaps it's just stuck in the hole in the path where it has been sitting."

"Let's try this, Victorious. Push the boulder gently -- just enough to get it to roll a few inches. Then let go all at once and stand back."

Victorious pushed. The rock rolled a few inches. Victorious let go. The rock rolled back a little bit past its original position, stopped, rolled the other way a smaller bit and then settled back to rest.

"See," said Niles, "it wobbles back and forth. It's dug itself a hole in the path and that's way it's so hard to roll. All we have to do is rock it gently, back and forth. Push, then let go. When it rolls back, push again."

Victorious understood perfectly. He pushed, let go, pushed again, let go again, and pushed again. Each time the boulder rolled a little further. "Now!" Niles yelled on the sixth push, and he and the bear shoved with all of their might.

With a deep thump, the boulder rolled out of its hole, turned over completely, balanced on what used to be its top, and then turned over again. When it came to rest there was clear space between the rock and the cliff wall. It was a tight squeeze for Victorious, but he handed Morning Gloria to Niles with a warning to be careful with her and pushed his way through.

Niles was dancing for joy, holding the flowerpot in one outstretched arm. "Careful," said Victorious in alarm, quickly retrieving his friend and then setting her down in a sunny spot under a tree limb. But he was just as pleased as Niles. Everyone was very happy. Someone began singing a song that began "Rock me gently." Niles didn't know the words, but it didn't matter.

"What a great feeling," observed Niles, "to solve a problem as hard as this one! Wow!"

I suppose you noticed that it was back to being a "problem" now. Once Niles had overcome it, that is.

Anyway, Niles felt great. Calamidrake felt lousy.

Chapter 19 - What a Crumby Thing to Happen

It was already dark, and a cool evening breeze blew off the river and across the path where Niles and his friends were standing. The tree branches above him swayed and rustled. The stars shone against a velvet background lit ever so slightly by a crescent moon in the east. Niles was tired, very tired, and very, very sleepy.

He wished for his bed, but wishing didn't make it appear. Wondering if he was going to have to sleep on the ground, Niles walked on, slowly and wearily. His friends kept up and said nothing.

"Frederick," he asked, "how do I make my bed appear? I'm very, very tired." He looked at the ferret but Frederick just shrugged. "I thought you could do anything," he chided with just a touch of unreasonableness in his voice.

Frederick didn't take offense. He answered simply: "I can't do anything for you that you can't do yourself." It wasn't the answer Niles wanted, but apparently it would have to do, so he just stumbled on, weary and resigned.

Just when he thought he would not be able to go even one step further, Niles remembered what Roger had told him. "Take one more step," his good friend had said, and each day Niles had done that. Somehow, drawing on reserves of energy he didn't even know he had, Niles managed to take another step, and then another, and finally one more.

And there it was! Thank goodness! His own comfortable, warm, cozy, and safe bed, sitting under a beautiful oak tree, with his blanket and pillow just where they ought to be.

"Flumpf!" That's the sound Niles made as he dropped down onto his bed with a sigh of contentment. His backpack slipped from his shoulder and came to rest on the side of the bed. His shoes were already loose so Niles had no trouble kicking them off. It felt so good to be in bed!

Victorious quietly came up on his right and handed Niles an old jelly jar now filled with cool water from the river. He heard someone (it was Claracuca) rummaging around in his backpack, and in a moment the iguana appeared with a large chocolate chip cookie that Niles had been saving for a special treat. One bite was missing and Claracuca looked a little embarrassed.

Gratefully, Niles took the cookie from Claracuca and thanked her. "You could have had a bigger bite than that," he told her.

"Really?" she replied, looking at him hopefully.

Niles laughed and broke off a piece of the cookie for her. He noticed Victorious by his side and Henrietta perched on the headboard above him. Of course, they should have a piece too. But where was that ferret?

Just then Niles felt a warm furry creature in bed beside him, brushing up against his back. Turning over he saw his best friend in the Endless Forest. Niles gave him a broad smile and tenderly stroked the lovely brown fur on the ferret's back. But Frederick paid no attention; he was too busy sniffing out and licking up the cookie crumbs that had fallen on the bed beside Niles!

Suddenly the ferret noticed that everyone was watching him. Stopping his ferreting, he looked up directly at Niles and said: "Well, you don't want to sleep on crumbs, do you?"

Henrietta hooted with delight. "Oh, you only ate the crumbs so that Niles could be more comfortable in bed, right?"

"Of course," answered Frederick. Henrietta hooted again. Victorious smiled. Claracuca flicked her tongue rapidly in all directions and smirked. Niles felt great affection for Frederick, who had helped him so much during the past three days and who had always made him smile when he needed it most. Breaking off half of what remained of the cookie, he offered it to the ferret.

You might think that Frederick hesitated for an instant before taking the cookie. Perhaps he wasn't sure if he should take so much of Niles' treat. That's what you might think, but I wouldn't. The cookie disappeared in a flash. "Delicious," Frederick managed to mumble between mouthfuls.

Crumbs flew everywhere. Even Henrietta had to shake herself vigorously to get clean. Presently the cookie was gone, except for hundreds of crumbs, most of which were on the bed next to Niles and Frederick.

"Aren't you going to eat those crumbs?" asked Henrietta. "To clean off the bed so Niles will be more comfortable?"

Frederick didn't even look up. Scratching his ear vigorously to shake off a couple of chocolate chips that were stuck in his fur, he just said "Nope. I'm not hungry anymore."

"Who's going to clean up the bed?" the owl demanded. Niles didn't want to get up - he was too comfortable and warm. Victorious came to the rescue. He gently slid Niles to one side of the bed. "Off!" he ordered the ferret, who had taken this opportunity to stretch out on the vacant half. Reluctantly, Frederick slid to the ground.

Claracuca had crept over to watch what was going on and to snag the occasional crumb that fell off the bed. Victorious bent down and carefully picked her up. "Hey, what are you doing?" the iguana snapped indignantly.

"Just be quiet and use your tail," ordered Victorious, holding Claracuca just above the empty half of the bed.

"My tail? What do you want me to do with my tail? ... Oh, I get it." And with a few swishes of her powerful tail, Claracuca soon had swept half of the bed clean of crumbs. Niles was amazed. With a little bit of cooperation there was no puzzle that he and his friends couldn't solve.

Niles shifted to the other side of the bed, and Victorious and Claracuca repeated their clean-up procedure on the remaining crumbs.

Now the bed was clean, and it was time to sleep. Niles settled snugly into the middle of his bed, with the blankets drawn over him up to his chin, and closed his eyes. "Flumpf!" Someone else plopped down in the bed beside Niles. It was Frederick of course. Niles made room for him under the covers and the ferret curled up next to his friend.

"Flumpf!" "Flumpf!" And then a flutter of wings, and one more "Flumpf!" All of his friends were in bed with him. Niles was amazed that they all fit. Victorious alone was far too big for his small bed, but now they were all nestled under the covers and no one seemed the least bit crowded.

For one brief moment, Niles felt Calamidrake in his mind. It seemed to chuckle and say "See you tomorrow" and then it was gone. Niles wondered what that could mean, but not for long. Sleep came quickly in the cool forest air, under a brilliant canopy of twinkling stars and wispy clouds backlit gently by the rising Moon.

Chapter 20 - When Is a Fish Not a Fish?

Niles awoke to Frederick's gentle snoring, although the ferret would forever deny it, and looked out on a beautiful morning. Early rays of the Sun slipped between tree trunks, branches, and leaves and created a pattern of light and dark all across the forest floor.

The first thing that Niles saw when he opened his eyes was a lovely patch of blue sky. It thrilled him. Until now the sky had always been gray in the Endless Forest. Niles had forgotten how beautiful colors could be. This morning he could see all kinds of colors, even some shades he never imagined.

The tree trunks were a rich deep brown and the leaves were dozens of different greens. The pine needles were a dark green tinged with gray, while the willow tree's long thin leaves were pale and nearly yellow in places.

Daisies with blue leaves and gold centers grew at the foot of the bed, and just beyond them Niles saw the trumpet-shaped flowers of both the white and the yellow honeysuckle. Curiously, there were still no reds and oranges. Niles wondered why. Thinking about these missing colors reminded him of the Dragon, and that reminded him of its threat (for that is what it now seemed to be). "See you tomorrow," it had said.

Other thoughts also gnawed at the corner of Niles' mind and made him uncomfortable. One was certainly about missing his parents, and another was wondering when this journey would be over. And what would life be like afterwards? And would his friends still be with him? Niles could not bear the thought of never seeing Victorious again, or Henrietta, or Claracuca, or most especially Frederick.

A tear grew in his eye and a mist lifted itself up all around him, partly hiding the trees, bushes, and flowers of the Endless Forest. Calamidrake yawned, uncurled its tail and spoke in a lazy way "Why did you come here anyway?"

"To get rid of you," Niles thought in answer.

"Really?" questioned the Dragon, now more awake. "I'm still here."

Niles didn't know what to say. Was there really any chance he could get Calamidrake out of his head forever? The entire journey was for the purpose of ridding himself from the Dragon. If he couldn't accomplish this, why go on?

Sensing Niles' uncertainty, the Dragon went on. "I've made a home here and have become a part of you. I am here to stay. I ask you again, 'Why did you come here?'" He seemed very smug this morning, considering that Niles had been able to control him every time he had appeared during the journey.

Niles knew that Calamidrake could not tell a complete lie. Although he certainly didn't trust the beast, Niles was becoming convinced on his own that this journey was pointless. As these thoughts grew in his mind, the Dragon began to change from green to yellow, and the tip of one wing turned orange.

Niles fidgeted in bed. Frederick's snoring had stopped, but the ferret was still lying motionless next to him, apparently asleep. Victorious, Henrietta, and Claracuca could be heard by the river, washing and searching for breakfast. Niles turned over to his side. His gaze fell upon the ground near a large oak tree, and sitting there was the flowerpot.

Morning Gloria's flowers were just opening in the morning light, each one blue and white and beautiful. She said nothing, but Niles could feel a power flowing into him. He remembered all of the lessons he had learned on the journey, and how they had given him the strength to overcome the Dragon and to solve other problems as well.

The journey no longer seemed pointless. Niles knew that it was drawing to a close, and he felt hopeful that its end would be a beginning as well. A bigger and better life awaited him at journey's end, and somehow all of his friends would be with him forever.

Niles stared at Morning Gloria and then he remembered. That was her magic -- to give hope. As he realized that, Calamidrake rapidly faded away. His last words echoed briefly through Niles' head. "I'll always be with you," and then he was gone.

"Baloney," thought Niles, but then he recalled that the Dragon couldn't tell him a complete untruth. "We'll see about that! Soon!" Niles exclaimed aloud.

The Endless Forest seemed to have a way of providing whatever Niles needed. He needed hope, and there was Morning Gloria. And he also still needed to know that his journey could succeed. "How," he thought, "can the Forest tell me that?" He would soon find out.

One thing Niles did know was that he was full of energy and eager to continue his journey. He felt strong. He felt courageous. He felt smart. He felt calm.

He felt hungry.

"Where's Victorious?" he muttered, since it was the bear who usually brought the food. Looking around, Niles could see no sign of Victorious, Henrietta, or Claracuca. Only Frederick was in sight, licking his paws lazily on the bed and occasionally stretching and yawning.

Niles remembered that he had heard splashing by the river and decided that was where his other friends must be. Perhaps they had some food. "Victorious" he called out. Then "Henrietta" and "Claracuca." When he got no answer, Niles started towards the river. The path did not go in that direction, but by carefully picking his way between bushes that always seemed to be directly in front of him, Niles gradually made his way.

He was already getting a little hot and sweaty, even though the morning was young and the air still cool, when he burst out of a particularly thick thicket of bristly bristle bushes. About fifty feet in front of him, he saw Victorious and Claracuca talking, apparently to the river.

As he got closer, Niles could hear the bear laugh and declare in his booming voice "That was the best one yet, Daniel." Henrietta, flying high over the river hooted her agreement and Claracuca splashed her tail in the water in delight, creating a shower of misty spray.

The river flowed gently at this point, and the breeze was not strong enough to raise even the smallest waves. Niles ran eagerly towards his friends, wondering who this Daniel was. Approaching, he saw riplets cascading outwards in expanding circles from a spot near the river's center. As he stood on the shore, wondering what could have made them, there was a sudden flash of silver. It broke through the surface of the water and rose to a height far over Niles' head.

With a shout of joy, Niles recognized the silver streak. It was a dolphin! A real dolphin like the ones he had seen on television. "This must be Daniel," he thought, as the sleek mammal reached the top of its flight and then, twisting and tumbling, fell back into the river with a thundering splash. Droplets of water reached all the way to the shore. Some even wet Niles' hair and shoes.

Claracuca slapped the water again with her tail and Henrietta hooted so hard that she forgot to flap her wings. She began to fall rapidly and for a moment it looked as if the owl would end up in the river. At the last second, she recovered, straightened out and soared across the shore, gaining height and eventually landing in a small overhanging tree.

Victorious greeted him.

"Hello, master Niles. Look who we found here.
I know you've been watching, of course.
Please come to the river; you need have no fear.
Yon Daniel's a good friend of ours.

He's been far away, 'til this very day --
His journey was finished and done.
It seems it's been years, I'm saddened to say.
We've missed him. So, Joy! that he's come.

The dolphin swam over to the shore to get a better look at Niles and rested his head just out of the water. "It does seem like a long time, but it has been only a little over one year," he said, never taking his large deep eyes off Niles. "So, this is the sojourner," he continued softly and thoughtfully, and then suddenly he addressed Niles himself: "Have you gotten much stronger?" he asked.

Niles was a bit taken aback. He had marveled at the dolphin's acrobatics and admired his lovely shiny silver skin, punctuated by pure white on his head and nose. But he really hadn't had a chance to get to know Daniel well and didn't feel comfortable talking about his journey. Still, Victorious had said that Daniel had been on a journey of his own. Obviously, he had finished it and was now free to come back to the Endless Forest just for a visit. It brought to mind a question that Niles just had to have answered.

"I think I have grown stronger," he said. "I've learned so many things about myself and about others that I don't know where to begin telling you."

"You could start at the beginning," interrupted Daniel. "Or sometimes the middle is best. The end can be good too."

Niles decided to get directly to the question that was bothering him. "I've been on this journey for four days now. Will it ever end? It's not that I'm not grateful -- everything and everyone has been wonderful -- but I miss my home and I'm sure my parents are missing me."

When Daniel did not answer immediately, Niles repeated his question: "Will my journey ever end?"

Daniel understood how Niles felt. Although his nature was to laugh and joke at everything, he now grew serious. "Yes, it will end. But whether your journey comes to a good end or a not-so-good one is up to you, and the matter is not yet decided. You will have to pass over the Bridge of Passage, and the Bridge will surely be guarded. It always is."

That sounded ominous to Niles. "The Bridge of Passage?" he asked. "What's that? Is that the end of the journey?"

But before Daniel could answer, Henrietta broke in. "No, Daniel, don't say too much. He must find out for himself."

Niles still looked hopefully at the dolphin, but Daniel just nodded his head sadly.

"Well, if you can't tell me about the Bridge, you can at least tell the story of your journey. It looks like it turned out well for you."

The smile reappeared on Daniel's face. "Oh, yes, I can tell you some things about that. Not everything of course. Maybe not even most things, but surely not nothing. Yes, 'something,' that's what I can tell you." Then he stopped talking and lay there at water's edge staring at Niles.

Frederick crept silently up to where Niles was standing and looked first at the boy and then at the dolphin. Abruptly he said "Ok, I'll tell the story ..."

Daniel slapped his tail hard on the water. This time the fountain of water he splashed shot directly towards Frederick. Only because the ferret was very quick on his feet did he avoid a complete soaking. "It's my story and I'll tell it." And he did.

Chapter 21 – Daniel Dolphin Tells No Lies

Speaking to all of them, but looking mostly at Niles, Daniel began. "I was a little older than you are -- that is, I was older in dolphin years, which are not quite the same as human years. But I was a very troubled mammal. The Dragon had a firm hold on me. Almost every day he appeared and told me terrible things about my friends and even about my mother and father. Worst of all, I listened and believed what he said.

"We lived in a very large pod. There was my mother, my father, my two older brothers, Zach and Mack, my two younger sisters, Ika and Lilah, and almost 40 other dolphins. We swam and played and fished together in the warm waters near Treasure Island, not too far from here."

Niles had been listening quietly, but now he just had to interrupt. "Treasure Island! Was there buried treasure -- gold and things like that?"

"I don't know about gold," answered Dan, "or about anything buried, but there were lots of delicious fish, warm currents, and excellent scratching rocks. It was a nice place to live, but I was making it miserable for my pod mates, especially my brothers.

"Once we were playing in Pirate's Cove. The Dragon had been pestering me all morning. At his suggestion, I hid behind some rocks and made noises like a killer whale. They eat dolphins you know.

I wasn't good enough to fool my brothers for long. They did get scared at first but soon they came back and scolded me. But I was good enough to lure a real killer whale. It came to investigate. We all had to swim for our lives. Luckily no one got caught, but we can never go back. And it was one of the prettiest places in the sea."

"Why can't you go back now?" asked Niles. "Surely the killer whale is gone."

"Killer whales never forget," answer Daniel regretfully.

Niles interrupted. "I thought that was elephants -- that never forget."

"What's an elephant?" asked Daniel. "I haven't seen any in the ocean."

Victorious thought that was funny, so he decided to show Daniel what an elephant was by getting up and acting like one. He stomped around like an elephant does (well, a little bit like an elephant does), and swung his head from side to side pretending to thrash an imaginary trunk in every direction. Daniel looked on with disbelief. Everyone else was laughing. Finally, Daniel said he understood. "An elephant is like a crazy bear, right?"

Niles was enjoying Victorious' clowning, but he was still interested in why the pod could never return to Pirate's Cove, so he asked again. "Why can't you go back?"

"Because killer whales never forget. It will come back to that cove from time to time, hoping to find dolphins. It's too dangerous. In fact, the pod considered leaving Treasure Island completely, but in the end, we decided to stay. I just hope no one is found by a killer whale." He fell silent.

Obviously, Daniel was sorry for the trouble he had caused and for the danger that threatened his pod because of it.

Everyone was quiet for a full minute. Niles felt he had to say something, but all he could think of was "It's sort of like the boy who cried wolf."

"No, it's not," answered Frederick, looking up from under a small bush where he was hunting, for nuts no doubt. "The boy who cried wolf kept doing it all the time until no one believed him; Daniel only acted like a killer whale once. They'll still believe him if he does it again."

"You can be sure I'll never do that again," the dolphin answered firmly. "But what's a wolf?"

Victorious began to get up again, but Henrietta hooted him down. "No! No more imitations." She flew down to Daniel and landed on his back. "A wolf is like a dog, but it's wild and sometimes hurts people." Daniel nodded.

While Henrietta was occupied explaining, Victorious got up. He was in a playful mood this morning and nothing could stop him. He began acting like a wolf, but I'm afraid that a huge bear and a wolf are so different in shape and in the way they are built, that Victorious didn't do a very good job. He did manage a nasty snarl that scared Claracuca, but everyone else just laughed.

In the distance, a wolf howled. That quieted them all down.

"Go on," Niles urged. "Go on with your story."

"Well," continued Daniel, "things were getting very bad for me. "The Dragon was out of control. One day, my oldest brother, Zach, swam over to me and told me it was time to take a journey."

"So, you came to the Endless Forest," Niles said.

"Yes, but dolphins need to stay in water, so we swim up the inlet into what you call a river. We just call it 'The Channel,' and usually nobody goes there because of all of the frightening tales. As you can see the trees overhang the water, almost covering it in places. Dolphins like the open ocean with sky overhead, going on forever in all directions. The Channel is not a place we would normally go. But I was desperate. I thought that I could lose the Dragon somewhere in the Channel and then go back home.

"Did you?" asked Niles anxiously. This was the one question to which he really needed an answer -- how could he finally get rid of Calamidrake and go home.

"No, of course not," answered the dolphin, "but that is one of the things I can't discuss with you."

Niles was shattered; if Daniel, who seemed to have had a successful journey, couldn't get rid of his Dragon, what hope did he have for himself? "I thought your journey was a success," he almost cried.

Daniel nodded his head vigorously and even slapped his tail to emphasize his answer. "It was! It was a big success. You'll see. Yours can be too. If only you don't give up."

Niles knew what Daniel meant by that! "I'll be careful not to say 'I quit' three times," he assured all of his friends.

"I'll bet the Dragon tried to get you to say that three times," said Daniel. "That was a nasty trick."

"A trick?!" Niles looked a little pale.

"Your journey will come to an end when you give up. That part is true. But you don't have to say anything. If you lose heart and stop trying, the journey ends. The Dragon was just trying to discourage you. I wonder how close he came. You could have gone back after saying 'I quit' twice, or even once, or even not at all. It all depends on how you felt inside. You must have kept a spark of courage alive or else you wouldn't be here now."

Henrietta broke in. "I think that's all you should say," the owl said sternly.

"Just one more question," pleaded Niles, and when no one said "No" right away, he asked it. "I'm supposed to cross a bridge soon and everyone seems to be worried about it. What dangers are going to be there?"

Daniel considered for a minute before answering. "I can tell you this much only. You must cross the bridge in order to complete your journey. There _are_ dangers there, and not all of them are in your mind. They cannot overcome you unless you let them. And that's all I can tell you. Besides, it's time for me to swim back to my pod. I came to say hello to Victorious and my other friends, and I have stayed too long already."

Daniel was just about out of sight, heading down the river or "Channel" as he called it. Niles thought about trying to shout out one more question, but just then a flash of lightening broke across the river downstream from the journeyers. A distant clap of thunder rolled and rumbled away into the trees.

His friends started to get nervous, Frederick especially. "It's time to move on," he urged Niles. "To go to the bridge." To emphasize the point, another lightening stroke lit the sky. This time the thunder was nearer and louder.

Chapter 22 - The Approach to the Bridge

The company started out hurriedly with frequent worried glances at the sky, now a deep ominous gray in the west. The path was winding and curvy in places but straight in others. It could change as quickly as the blink of an eye. Some parts were smooth, while in others rocks made the going difficult.

Niles noticed that he was getting out of breath, probably because the path was very steep. But whatever pace he chose, slow or fast, his friends kept to it easily. Even Claracuca, the deliberate iguana, could scurry as quickly as Frederick.

At one point the path leveled and there was a convenient place to rest -- a fallen log on a grassy but dry hillock. Niles gratefully sat down for a few moments, but not for very long. Any time the party stopped to rest for too long, ugly gray clouds began to build, the wind picked up, and the flashes and crashes of the oncoming storm became insistent, persistent, and threatening. But if the travelers kept a fast pace, the storm came no nearer; the thunder and lightening even seemed to lessen. There was only one thing to do; they had to move as quickly as possible forward, towards the Bridge of Passage.

Aside from being tired, though, Niles was in fine spirits. He didn't let the weather or the obstacles on the path bother him too much. In fact, on one particular steep climb, he began to sing:

> Is it a mountain
> Or is it a hill?
> Will we all climb it
> Or will we stand still?

To which Morning Gloria answered. "That depends on how you look at it." Well, that was something new! In fact, it was two somethings new. Morning Gloria (now snuggled securely in the crook of Victorious' massive arm) had spoken! What is more, her flowers were open even though it was already past noon. Perhaps this was because they were nearing the Bridge of Passage, where all of the powers of the Endless Forest came together.

Gazing at Morning Gloria gave hope, as it always had for Niles, and he changed his song slightly:

> Is it a mountain
> Or is it a hill?
> No matter how high,
> Climb it we will!

Actually, the sight of Morning Gloria did even more for Niles. He was now totally "awake," aware of everything about him -- the colors, sounds, smells, and shapes of the forest. Even his emotions had become like tangible things and foremost among them Niles recognized joy, the joy that came from the companionship of such remarkable friends.

They were traveling rapidly now, outrunning even the storm. As they topped the mountain, the Sun came out from behind the clouds. A beautiful vista spread out in front of them. Waterfalls seemed to come from nowhere and cascade to unseen depths just beside their path. One actually fell from a large rock that jutted out directly over Niles' head! Then the falling stream smacked against a patch of large gray stone only ten feet to their left, while the sunlight shining through the mist made fairy-like rainbows appear and disappear above them.

Claracuca found a rock just out of the reach of the stream and sunned herself with exclamations and sighs of pure pleasure. Morning Gloria was absorbing the fine clear spray on her flowers, and Frederick ran from rock to rock, poking his nose into anything that looked interesting and muttering something like "Better than nuts. Better than berries." Hmm, interesting little creature, that ferret.

Victorious came and sat on a dry rock next to Niles, where they both could hear the sounds and smell the freshness of clean, cool refreshing running water. They knew they could not stay long, nor could they cut the experience short, since this was a day of intense joy and pleasure swirling beside and among the anxiety about what was to come.

Too soon, it was time to start out. Niles noticed that several smaller paths branched off the main one. Victorious suggested a narrow but well-worn pathlet which led to many of his favorite beehives. There would be lots of honey there, he told Niles. Claracuca preferred a stony one where she expected to find warm, sunny rocks. Henrietta had no favorite, but she flew over them all and said that the one that headed directly east was lined with berry bushes and nut trees. Frederick immediately proclaimed that was the path he would choose.

But the final decision belonged to Niles, since it was his journey, and for him there was really no choice. He knew the main path was the one he needed to take. Although he would have liked to make his friends happy by exploring each of their favorite ways, this was not the time. Niles had learned to choose, taking into account the needs and wants of his companions and himself, and in the end picking the right option. He didn't think about it in these terms, but Niles had grown very strong.

He would need to be, because the party had not gone fifty steps before the Bridge came into view.

I don't know how to describe the Bridge of Passage, because each person sees it differently. To Niles it was a short span of great gray stones. The path emerged from the trees about forty steps from the Bridge and ran through a flat grassy space until it came to within just a few steps of the river. There, a small hill partly covered by a strange bush with yellow leaves and green flowers hid the entrance to the Bridge.

The Bridge itself arched upward sharply to cross the River, which although not wide at this point, it was very, very deep and flowed very swiftly. Even from a distance they could hear the water smack against the stone columns that supported the bridge and hurry away into the distance. There were no sides to the bridge; anyone crossing it would have to be very careful to keep to the center and to avoid falling into the rushing waters.

On the far side, the Bridge ended in deep shadows cast by a huge rock. Then the path ran off unhindered into a stand of oak trees and disappeared.

Niles stopped and stared at the Bridge. Somehow, he knew that this was his final test. But he could not figure out what the test would be. The bridge was narrow, but not too narrow; there did not seem to be much danger of falling into the river (unless, of course, something pushed him). He had secretly believed that the wolves they had heard howling the night before would be waiting for him at the Bridge, but there was no sign of them, unless they were hiding behind the bush or the large rock on the other bank.

He looked to his friends. Niles was sure they knew a lot about the Bridge, but he was also sure they wouldn't tell him very much. Well, just maybe he could get them to say something. "I don't see anything dangerous," he suggested.

But he got no response. "It looks like we can just walk across the Bridge. No problem at all." Still his friends were silent, but looking at them he could tell they didn't think it would be that easy.

"You're supposed to be my friends," he said now, feeling scared. "Tell me what you know!" His voice was loud, sharp, and demanding. Victorious just looked away. Perched on a low branch, Henrietta eyed him sadly. Claracuca slid off of the path and lost herself in some low bushes.

Frederick was the only one who spoke. He came up to Niles and rubbed against his leg reassuringly. "You can do it," he said. "You've come this far and you've become very strong. You can do it."

But this didn't satisfy Niles. He needed to know exactly what was waiting for him on the Bridge. Or was it _on the way to_ the Bridge? He had suddenly noticed that there were several stretches of the path ahead which were hidden by trees, rocks, or small hills. Something could be hiding behind any one of them. But were they even there when he had last looked? Niles couldn't remember.

He glanced at the sky. The storm was coming closer. A clap of thunder boomed to his left, while unseen lightening sent flickering shadows across the path in front of him. Could the storm pose a threat?

"Tell me what the danger is!" he exclaimed desperately. When they didn't answer, he just muttered "Ok, I'll just have to find out myself."

And so, Niles stepped back onto the path and began walking briskly towards the Bridge. His mind was sharp and clear. He could overcome whatever it was that waited for him. He didn't need his friends. They weren't even in his mind. But something else was.

"Hi, pal," hissed Calamidrake.

Chapter 23 - The Last Battle

Niles had not expected that voice, and the shock took his breath away. His heart started thumping so hard he could actually see it pounding in his chest. "Oh, no," he thought, "not now!"

But Niles didn't have very long to worry about the Dragon, for he had come abruptly upon a very steep wall. It seemed to appear from out of nowhere, but there it was, tall and gray and smooth and right in the middle of the path. There was a small opening leading directly towards the Bridge. Niles turned quickly to his right, but as soon as he did another wall appeared, just as steep and dark and menacing as the first. No matter where he turned, Niles' progress was blocked. The only direction he could go was back along the path, in the direction from which he came, or forward toward the bridge.

Niles knew that to retreat would mean the end of his journey and total failure. He remembered what Daniel had told him: "Your journey will come to an end when you give up. It all depends on how you feel inside."

To make matters worse, the storm was suddenly all around him. Thunder and lightning lashed the air. Large drops of rain spattered onto the path. Niles began to get frantic. He quickly decided that he really did need his friends' help, but when he looked about, they were nowhere to be seen. "Where are you?" he wailed, but only to himself. Fear had taken away Niles' ability to speak, so his pleading "Please help me" was lost within his lonely thoughts.

"They can do nothing for you that you can't do for yourself," came the mocking voice of the Dragon. It was reading his thoughts.

And that was the moment when everything became clear to Niles, or at least he thought it did. Calamidrake could read his thoughts! Just like Frederick, Victorious, Henrietta, Claracuca and even the river Itasara.

Even more startling is what the Dragon had said: "They can do nothing for you that you can't do for yourself." That was almost exactly what Frederick had said to him yesterday when he asked his friend to make his bed appear. "How could he know to say the same thing that Frederick had?" Were all of his friends really friends of Calamidrake!? Did they bring him here just so the Dragon could utterly destroy him?

Niles was in a panic and not thinking clearly at all. Because if his brain was working normally, he would have figured out that Calamidrake could have heard what Frederick said the night before and simply repeated it. It is very easy to get the wrong idea and then to act foolishly, particularly when you are scared and wet and alone in the Endless Forest. But when you panic, your brain definitely does not work right.

"Oh, no! no! no!" Niles screamed, suddenly finding his voice. "They're in it with you! All of them - Frederick, Victorious, Henrietta -- all of them. They tricked me. They lured me here." But there was still doubt in his mind. Even as he said the words, Niles wondered if they were true. Could he have been so wrong? Could all of his friends really be enemies in disguise?

Things looked very bleak, and to tell the truth, the only reason Niles didn't turn and flee back up the path and give up his journey was that his legs weren't paying any attention to his brain at the moment. They just stood there, and so the rest of him did too.

The Dragon moved in for the "kill."

It had grown very large now and seemed to be outside of Niles' mind altogether. It appeared to be sitting on top of the weird yellow and green bush on the hill near the entrance to the Bridge. Colored entirely a brilliant red (except for its head), Sir Draconis of the Ugly-Thoughts whipped its tail from side to side with sharp snaps that were almost as loud as the thunder that shrieked from the black clouds overhead. Steam shot from both nostrils in a steady blast. Its eyes whirled with flecks of orange and red mixed into a burning yellow.

Niles' strength was ebbing. His will to continue was almost gone, and Calamidrake would soon have had a victory until it made a mistake. Villains always seem to commit one error. Perhaps this is to give good people like Niles the chance to pull themselves out of any depth to which they have fallen. The world does not ask of us more than we can do.

Patience would have probably been enough, but the Dragon tried to hasten Nile's retreat by talking. "Nonsense, your friends wouldn't do anything to hurt you. You did it all to yourself. If you had learned what you should have, you would be strong enough to win our battle on the Bridge of Passage."

Do you see the mistake? I admit it is not a very obvious one, but it is there nonetheless. Still Calamidrake was very smart, and it also planted a nasty trap in that short speech. Niles missed the mistake, but he fell for the trap, as you shall see.

A particularly bright stroke of lightening flashed directly behind the Dragon, illuminating it against a background of dark trees. The lightening might have scared Niles, but it didn't. In the brief instant between it and the deafening thunder that followed, Niles saw the Dragon as a small creature, at least as compared to the tall pines of the Endless Forest. It wasn't much, but it did give him a little hope. And that was what Niles needed most desperately.

He turned what the Dragon had said over in his mind. He had denied that his forest friends had betrayed him, but what would you expect him to say about his own spies. More than ever Niles was convinced that Henrietta, Victorious, Claracuca, and even Frederick were part of Calamidrake's plot.

Apparently, there was to be a battle on the Bridge of Passage. He would have to fight the Dragon. What chance did he have?

It is very much to Niles' credit that he at least thought about finding a weapon. His courage was not completely gone, nor his hope, and as long as these remained, the journey would continue and Niles would have that chance. But what weapon would work against a huge dragon with a murderous tail and scalding steam that he could hurl twenty feet in front of him? And that is not to even mention the armor all over its body, its rows of sharp teeth, and claws that could shred any branch Niles might find.

Calamidrake read all of these thoughts. It was having a marvelous time. As if to confirm everything that Niles was thinking, it reached down and uprooted a fifteen-foot oak tree. Clasping it tightly in one clawed fist, it raked it with the other. Leaves and branches flew everywhere and soon nothing was left of the tree but heaps of Dragon-sized toothpicks. Calamidrake might have used one of these to pick its teeth but it was having too much fun shooting sprays of steam out to singe and wither the falling leaves that filled the air.

Searching for any weapon that might give him a chance, Niles slowly approached the bridge. The black walls would let him go directly forward or backward, but they blocked every other direction. Niles looked towards some fallen branches on his left, thinking that the Dragon would surely just make toothpicks of them too, when he stumbled on something hard.

It was the tip of a rock protruding a few inches from the path, but the thing that caught Niles' attention was that it was very sharp! Eagerly he bent down to dig it out of the path, but it was buried deeply and the dirt was dry and unyielding.

Meanwhile, Calamidrake had jumped down from its perch and taken a position squarely in the center of the Bridge of Passage. "Come on, come on. Or the rain will get you before I do." His voice was filled with command. Niles felt drawn towards him, but he had to have a weapon!

Digging frantically, Niles felt the pull of the storm's wind drive him directly towards the Bridge. The rain beat down in sheets, cold but unable to wash off the sweat pouring from his forehead. At the last possible moment, when Niles felt that he could not delay the battle one moment longer, the dirt gave way and the rock was in his hand.

It was large and dark gray, but it seemed to glitter whenever the lightening flashed. In desperation, Niles hoped that some kind of Forest magic was in it. Cautiously, he approached the Bridge and took two hesitant steps onto it. The black walls fell away behind him; the river itself was enough of a barrier.

The Bridge felt hard and unforgiving beneath Niles' feet. It was paved with rocks very much like the one that was in his hand, although the Bridge's, of course, were much larger. And now, Niles was faced with another problem. The rock was heavy. He could barely carry it in one hand. His plan had been to get as close to the Dragon as possible and then to heave the rock at his head, but now Niles wondered if he could throw it that far.

It was a forlorn hope anyway, but Niles had read about David and Goliath, and he refused to give up. The Dragon waited impatiently, stomping its feet and scorching the raindrops that fell around it until they evaporated into tiny puffs of mist. It seemed to be playing a game, trying to keep the raindrops off his feet. Calamidrake was not even taking Niles seriously!

He crept as close to the Dragon as he dared, staying just out of range of the searing steam that could kill him in a second. Then, mustering all of his courage and all of his strength, he levered the rock back over his head and flung it at the Dragon.

No other boy his size could have thrown that rock so hard, but Niles was motivated by the knowledge that this was his last chance. If he failed, so would his journey fail, and that meant that Calamidrake would rule his life until the day Niles died.

Upward the rock soared, truly aimed at the point of the Dragon's nose. The Dragon didn't even seem to see it, or else he just didn't care. In any case, after long moments that seemed as if they would never end, the rock struck.

With a thud, the rock bounced off Calamidrake's nose and dropped with a splash into the raging river below. For a moment, Niles thought that he had won. The Dragon stopped steaming and took a deep shuddering breath. Had he killed it? Niles dared to hope.

And then, the Dragon laughed. It was the loudest and most terrible laugh Niles had ever heard. It hadn't been injured at all, not in the slightest. The only reason the steam had stopped was so that it could draw in enough breath for that hideous laugh!

Niles knew it was over. The last spark of hope was fading fast in his breast. In the past, the situation had seemed hopeless, but one of his friends had always appeared with just enough help to save him. But now they were gone -- worse yet, probably agents of his enemy.

This is when Henrietta spoke. In a tone so authoritative that it could not be ignored, she asked: "Niles, what do you see ahead of you?"

For just a moment, the owl's commanding voice drowned out Calamidrake and even the thunderstorm. "Look carefully. Do you see an obstacle, or do you see an opportunity?"

Niles looked about frantically for Henrietta, but she was nowhere to be seen. "What could she possible mean?" he wondered. Momentarily, the owl had given him hope, but it faded as rapidly as it rose. "It's probably just another one of the Dragon's tricks," he thought.

Nonetheless, Niles did what the owl had ordered. "What do I see? Well, there's Calamidrake, about thirty feet high and right in the middle of the Bridge. If I approach him, he'll rip me to pieces, and if I stay here, sooner or later he'll come get me. I have no choice. I have to go back. That's all I see."

Even in despair, Niles' heart ran ahead of his brain. He could not completely believe that his forest companions had not really been his friends. He had learned trust and it would not die until he did. "Forgive me, Henrietta," Niles said, starting to turn back. "Forgive me, Victorious and Claracuca and Frederick, my dear ferret."

That was the beginning of the end for Calamidrake. And it knew it. "Come on, wimp" he roared, beating his chest with a clenched fist. But Niles was beginning to awaken.

"They were always my true friends!" he exclaimed, both delighted and overwhelmed with the realization. The Dragon had said "your friends wouldn't do anything to hurt you," and that had been his mistake, because Calamidrake could not tell Niles a complete lie. So, it must have been true. His friends would not do anything to hurt him!

Now he knew that Henrietta was on his side, and Niles concentrated hard on her words. "Do you see an obstacle, or an opportunity?" she had asked. "Well," he said out loud, "I certainly see an obstacle. It's hard to miss that awful Dragon! But an opportunity? ..."

He puzzled over it. There must be an opportunity there. Somewhere.

Then, like a flash of lightening going off in his head, Niles knew. "Of course, there's an opportunity. If I can get across the Bridge, I'll win and the Dragon will have to go away. That's what Henrietta meant."

Niles studied the Bridge again. Calamidrake was still firmly anchored to its center, its wings spread out from one edge of the Bridge to the other. It was shouting and cursing at him now, calling him every name it could think of and threatening to come get him if he didn't approach and fight.

Looking around him, Niles saw no other way to cross the river. Swimming was impossible. The river raged with a force that even the strongest swimmer couldn't challenge, and Niles could just barely swim across the school's pool. The dark walls that had sprung up when he first saw the Dragon would reappear if Niles left the bridge, and cut off every other direction except back, and that is the one way Niles refused to go.

There might be another way across the river, but Niles couldn't find it, so it had to be the Bridge. And that meant the Dragon.

Clearly, he couldn't fight the beast. He had taken his best shot with the sharp rock and the only damage it had done to Calamidrake was to cause it to choke on its own laughter for a few seconds.

And that, you see, had been the Dragon's trap -- it had said that Niles was not "strong enough to win" a battle and Niles had taken that to mean that there had to be a fight. All of his life, Niles had fought when faced with a challenge, so this was natural to him, and Calamidrake had taken advantage of it. But the Dragon had never said there had to be a fight at all. It was too bad that Niles hadn't figured that out yet.

Shivering from cold and fright, Niles looked for some other way. Perhaps he could run past it. But how? The Dragon blocked the Bridge completely, as best as Niles could tell in the darkness.

As he was thinking, Niles crept slowly closer. Now he was within range of the deadly blasts of steam and, in another few steps, the Dragon would be able to reach out with its claws and slash him, or push him off the Bridge to certain death below. But the Dragon did nothing, except to call names, curse, and threaten.

A brilliant stroke of lightening lit the sky for a few short seconds. It was time enough for Niles to see that the Dragon's wing did not reach quite to the left edge of the Bridge. There was room to squeeze by, barely. But the stones were wet and slippery, and Niles was afraid he would misstep and plunge into the deadly water.

"Why am I afraid of that?" thought Niles. "I'll never get that far anyway." Still, it was his best plan - creep as close to the Dragon as he dared and then make a mad dash, as fast as his feet would take him, right along the left edge of the Bridge. It wasn't a very good plan, but I doubt you could have come up with a better one under the circumstances.

As you recall, the first part of the plan was to creep as close to the Dragon as he could. Niles decided that would be just out of range of the sharp claws. He was almost there already. One more step and he would have to run.

He took that step.

"Run, run," Niles told his legs, but nothing happened. Fear and anxiety had taken away their strength. For a moment, Niles remained frozen, but then, from somewhere deep inside of himself in a place that most of us never go, he found one more ounce of courage. Enough to take one more step. And then one more. And another, and another, and another.

He was within just a few feet of Calamidrake. Suddenly, he turned his head, lowered it to Niles' level, and looked directly at him. Its red-hot nostrils shot steaming spray just over Niles' head. When it spoke, its roar shook the rocks of the Bridge itself. Threats and oaths stormed out of its mouth, but nothing it said shook Niles as much as its last sentence. In a voice filled with anger and despair, it concluded: "I will always be with you."

"I guess that's true," thought Niles, "but I'm not going to worry about it now." It was all he could do to force his feet to move one step further along the Bridge, to the narrowest point where the Dragon's wing reached nearly to the edge of the Bridge itself. At any moment, Calamidrake could stop playing with him and thrust him into the river, or pick him up in his jaws, or rip him with his claws.

But he didn't.

"Why haven't you killed me?" screamed Niles, with a defiance born of desperation. But Calamidrake didn't answer.

And then Niles finally understood.

The Dragon <u>didn't</u> kill him because the Dragon <u>couldn't</u> kill him. It was all bluff. His only weapon was his voice, and when Niles stopped paying attention to that, the Dragon became as harmless as a dream.

Niles would never be able to recall crossing the rest of the Bridge, or seeing his friends gather around him on the far side. The storm ended, but Niles didn't remember it rushing off into the distance, leaving a bright Sun, drying stones, and only an occasional drip of rain falling from the oak leaves. Would he remember the bright colorful rainbow?

He would remember Calamidrake, now small and pale blue, still standing on the center of the Bridge, and he would remember his last words, repeated over and over again: "I'll always be with you." But these were now said softly and with indescribable sadness.

Niles stood up straight. He looked taller than his true height and his voice was strong and unwavering. "I know. You will be with me, but I'll be in control. You have a job to do, like a watchdog. You will warn me when I'm starting to get upset about something, and when I hear you, I'll know it's time to stop and figure out what *I* really want to do."

The Dragon didn't say any words, but it howled in its sorrow and pain, and curled his tail around himself as tightly as he could, trying to disappear.

Such was the compassion that Niles had learned in the Forest that he didn't like to see any creature in pain - not even Calamidrake. "Don't worry," he said, "it won't be so bad. You can learn to do other things, maybe. And we'll _all_ be together back at my home."

He looked fondly at his friends when he said this last, but they looked away and didn't meet his eyes. "Oh, no!," thought Niles despairingly, "we will all be together. Won't we?"

Chapter 24 - Many Leave Takings

Niles was not just tired, he was exhausted. All he could do was collapse on the grass that grew tall and sweet by the banks of the river. That the grass was still wet from the rain didn't bother him at all. Comforted by the soft green blanket, Niles fell into a dreamless, untroubled sleep.

When he awoke it was well past noon. The Sun in the west hovered just above the tops of tall pine trees, which cast their shadows over the grass, the path, and most of the river. There were no clouds in the sky and just a hint of a soft southerly breeze.

Niles' friends were all around him. Even Henrietta, who almost always perched on a tree or at least a large bush, was standing on the ground. Niles looked around and saw smiling faces in all directions. His gaze fell on Frederick, who had given him friendship and support throughout the journey. Frederick smiled back at Niles but made no move to come over to him.

Niles' attention turned to Victorious and Morning Gloria who had shared with him their weaknesses and strengths, allowing him to recognize his own. Then on to Henrietta, who had taught him wisdom. And, finally, to Claracuca who had shown him the joy that could be found in just being a part of the Earth. All of his friends returned his gaze, and all were smiling, but none of them said anything.

I am sure you see the problem here. Niles' journey was drawing quickly to a close. Everyone knew it and nobody wanted to say goodbye. Especially Niles. He had conquered his Dragon and even turned it in to a guard to tell him when his emotions might be getting out of control. The purpose of his journey was finished and now it was time to end it and go home.

Unfortunately, Niles didn't know how to find his way back home. So, he did the logical thing - he asked his friends. And, if he directed his question a little more towards Henrietta than the others, who could blame him. The owl had saved him at the Bridge of Passage. She always seemed to have the right answers. He asked simply: "Does anyone know how I can get home?"

"Whose home are you talking about?" came a reply, but none of his friends had spoken a word. Niles looked around to find the source of the new voice; it seemed familiar but he couldn't quite identify it. "If you mean my home, then you are already here. But if it's Victorious' home you mean, that would be in many places, some of them close and others quite far away."

The speaker was Itasara, of course. She was the river beside which they had been walking, which was part of the Slow River, also known as Flusso and Profondo, and by many other names as well.

Niles turned to face the river, although it was quite impossible to tell exactly from where the voice came. His question about going home had not been answered, but as usual he had many more questions and could not resist trying at least one of them.

"Then it was you underneath the Bridge. If I had fallen, would you have killed me?"

"Could I kill myself?" came the answer.

Niles had no idea what Itasara meant. "What does that have to do with it?" he countered.

"You have just begun to understand," the river replied. "I am part of you and you of me. I don't read your thoughts - I _am_ your thoughts. In the Endless Forest, thoughts, feelings, and dreams give shape to things that you can see and touch. As you learned about the Forest and its creatures, you were actually learning about your own emotions and needs."

Niles thought he understood a little of this. It was like a dream in a way. "You're not real, then," he stated.

Itasara chuckled. "I'm real, Niles," she said. "As real as you are. Put your foot into my current and it will get wet. Not 'dream' wet, but really truly wet. The Endless Forest is a real place. Don't you remember that you knew about it long before your journey began?"

That was true, but Niles was having trouble understanding how Itasara could be real on one hand, and part of him on the other. He didn't really expect to get an understandable answer from the river, but perhaps

Henrietta could explain. Then a thought struck him. "If Itasara is part of my thoughts, then Henrietta ..."

"Yes! Yes!" hooted the owl, hopping up and down on one foot excitedly. "Now you have it. We are all part of you, but we all have lives of our own too. I have a home near the Scaly Mountains on the other side of the Forest -- a fine nest with a mate and two eggs that are ready to hatch. And Victorious has a roomy den -- actually a cave, and Claracuca has a tree home with sunny exposures every day of the year. We're all real, but in the Endless Forest, you can see parts of yourself in each of us. Now you understand, don't you?"

Niles didn't want to admit that he was still quite confused. What it seemed to amount to was that creatures in the Endless Forest acted like mirrors. But instead of showing his body, they showed him parts of his mind. There was obviously much more to it, but that was enough for Niles ... for now. "Yes, I understand," he answered. Henrietta nodded happily.

By now you may think that Niles had forgotten about his original question -- the one about how to get home, but Niles rarely forgets questions. And he still wanted to know: "How do I get home?"

Of all of the people who would have answered, Niles least expected Claracuca, but it was the iguana who spoke up. "Ending the journey is up to you. You could have quit by just giving up, but you didn't. Now that you have reached your goal, you can end the journey by simply thinking that it is over."

That makes sense, you must admit. It certainly did to Niles, but he was not quite ready to leave the Endless Forest. He was not ready because leaving the forest also meant leaving his friends. True, they were "part of him," but he would miss them actually being beside him and talking with him and snuggling into bed together at night.

"I know I have to go back," he said, "and my parents must be frantic with worry, but I don't want to leave you."

"It is the way," said Henrietta. "You must. But I wouldn't be too concerned about your mother and father. Time in the Endless Forest is different from time in the rest of the world. When you return, you will find that only a small part of a day has passed."

Victorious had been silent up until now, but he recognized the pain Niles was feeling. His words echoed within Niles, comforting him and filling him with hope.

Don't be sad,
Little lad.
Things are never quite so bad
As they seem
In a dream,
where you wander by the stream.

Eer we go,
Don't you know,
Each will give you something so
That you'll be
Constantly

Feeling them ... and also me!

Why can say,
Here today,
When your path returns this way?
All or one,
Missing none!
There will surely be great fun!

"I'll go first," the bear continued, "because I'm getting hungry and it's a long walk back to my den. I made this for you a couple of days ago." From a basket he had been carrying, Victorious pulled out a flat branch. The bark had been stripped away and the surface ground smooth. Dug into the wood were the words 'Never Dare a Bear!' He gave it to Niles.

Niles didn't know what to say. It was a lovely gift and would always remind him how Victorious had shown him the foolishness of taking dares. As he bent to put the treasure away in his now almost empty knapsack, Niles realized that he wanted to give Victorious something too. But what? He rummaged around in his backpack, but there wasn't much there. Finally, at the very bottom and underneath a spare shirt, he found the perfect gift. It was a jar of peanut butter -- extra crunchy. Hmm, he thought he had run out of peanut butter and was delighted to have found this one.

Victorious was astounded. In our world, a jar of peanut butter might not be very special, but the Endless Forest has no grocery stores, so peanut butter is rare indeed.

"It's perfect!" exclaimed Victorious. "My cubs have never had peanut butter. Thank you. Thank you very much."

He turned to go, but immediately returned and said sheepishly "I forgot about Morning Gloria." Niles had been hoping that he might take the plant back home and grow it in his garden, but obviously Victorious was not about to give up his treasure.

"I have something for you, too," came a small voice from within the flowerpot. A single stalk began to grow from Morning Gloria's center. When it reached a little more than a foot high, one flower grew and blossomed. It was perfect -- blue with a pure white center. As Niles watched, the flower opened and then, after a very brief time, began to close. Its petals withered and fell off. All that remained was a small clump of seeds hanging onto the stalk where the white center of the flower had been. This, then, was Morning Gloria's gift to Niles. Slowly and carefully, he reached down and gathered the seeds, putting then gently into his handkerchief, which he then folded together and slipped into his back pocket.

Niles could think of nothing to give to Morning Gloria. He stroked her leaves tenderly and said a few words "I'll always remember you." But that was enough, because all that 'Hope' needs to grow is fertile soil (which Victorious supplied every morning) and someone who cares. Many times, the best gift is something you do or say. Niles understood that now, and he realized that even in these last few hours, the Endless Forest had lessons to teach.

Now it was time for Victorious and Morning Gloria to leave. Niles could hardly manage to look, but he did voice a weak "Goodbye."

"Farewell," answered the bear, already disappearing into the depths of the Endless Forest. "Live long," he called back. "And prosper," added Morning Gloria.

The forest seemed empty without the huge and gentle bear and his flowerpot of hope. But Niles had their gifts, and he was very much looking forward to seeing his mother and father again. Of course, Claracuca, Henrietta, and, especially, Frederick were still with him, and the four friends wandered slowly through the forest, following a path that was now straight and wide with brilliant displays of flowers and blooming bushes on all sides.

They had only gone a short way when Claracuca stopped and sniffed at a faint path that branched to the right. "This is _my_ way home," she said simply. "The day is fading, and I would like to reach my warm bed before it gets too cold outside."

The iguana looked slyly at Niles and deliberately slapped her long wide tail on a dusty spot in the path. Dirt flew everywhere and Niles jumped back to avoid getting covered with it. "This is my gift," said Claracuca.

"Thanks," said Niles dubiously, brushing dirt off of his shirt and pants.

Claracuca thought that was very funny. She slapped her tail into the ground several more times. As Niles was beginning to wonder if it was possible for iguanas to lose their minds, his friend stopped chortling long enough to explain. "Scoop up some of this dirt and take it with you. When you plant Morning Gloria's seeds, put some of it in with them. Remember, hope needs fertile soil in which to grow."

Slapping her tail three more times, Claracuca slipped off into the brush and vanished with hardly a sound. Niles had no time to give her a gift, but what can you give to a friend who is the Earth itself?

Niles had just had time to fill an empty walnut shell with dirt, wrap it with leaves and tie it with a piece of honeysuckle vine, when he heard another voice, Itasara's. "Your path flows no longer by my waters, so I too will say farewell to you now. Fill your empty jelly jar with my water, and use it to wet the ground in which you plant Morning Gloria's seeds. Be very careful -- you have no idea how precious a gift those were."

Niles did what Itasara told him. Standing by the banks of the slowly flowing river, he couldn't help but cry. Seven tears fell one by one from his cheeks into the deep waters.

To this day, the wiser animals of the Endless Forest tell that the tears did not mix with Itasara's water, nor did they get carried out to sea with the rest of her flood. Instead, they remain in a small pool that sits in a quiet spot under a huge willow tree, where Itasara runs especially slowly, and where the spirit of the river itself draws inspiration and power from the reminder of Niles' courage.

In such a way does man give back to the world just as he draws from it.

That left just Henrietta and Frederick, both of whom watched silently as Niles said his last goodbye to the mighty river. When he turned back to them, they could see conflicting emotions in his eyes. Leaving his new friends was very hard, but going home meant reuniting with many old ones, especially Roger. If only Victorious, Morning Gloria, and Claracuca could have stayed with him, everything would be perfect. But Niles knew that was impossible.

He still hoped, however, that Frederick might come with him. That had been his idea since the second day, when the ferret had told Niles that he would like to have a home like the one in which Niles lived. Maybe there was still a way.

Minutes passed. Niles really didn't know what to do, so he did what came naturally to him -- he asked a question: "Can't I just stay here forever?"

When that got no answer, he thought of another: "How do you know your eggs are about to hatch, Henrietta? And who's watching them while you're with us?"

Henrietta hooted with laughter, and taking off with two strong steps, glided in circles over Niles' head. Frederick was rolling on the ground in hysterics. "Hoot," said the owl, "you'll never stop asking questions, will you?"

Niles couldn't help laughing with them. Presently his gloom lifted and he understood that the forest had given him a parting gift -- one last lesson. "It doesn't do much good to feel sorry for yourself," he remarked to no one in particular.

"No, it doesn't," said a deep booming voice which seemed to come from all directions.

"Does even the Forest have a voice?" Niles exclaimed.

"No that was me. Hugh. Remember? I'm the moose you met your first day in the Endless Forest." And there he was in front of them, standing directly on their path looking Niles squarely in the eye. But before Niles could think of anything to ask, he was off, bouncing through the forest, singing (of course) "The moose is loose ... the moose is loose."

Niles realized that the time for the last goodbyes had come. Henrietta spoke first. "Yes, it is time. And to answer your last questions, a mother owl always knows when it's time for her eggs to hatch, and my mate, Sunnio, is taking very good care of them, I promise you. I have a gift for you too and here it is." From the owl's claw dropped a small rock, about the size of golf ball, but perfectly clear and round.

Niles picked it up and stared at it. "Is this a magic crystal ball?" he asked.

"No," chuckled Henrietta. "It's a rock. We call it quartz, although it isn't even as big as a pint. But it is very clear, and if you hold it so the Sun shines through it, a rainbow will appear."

Fortunately, the Sun was shining, so Niles tried out his new gift at once. It was just as Henrietta had said. The sunlight broke up into all colors after passing through the quartz, and, shining on the path behind him, colored it with a brilliant rainbow.

"Now that you have succeeded in your journey, you can see and appreciate all of the colors of the world," Henrietta explained. "Even reds and oranges, which were hidden from you until you mastered your Dragon! Perhaps you will remember me also sometimes. And now, goodbye."

"No, wait!" cried Niles. "I want to give you something too. I've been thinking about it, and now that you're about to become a mother, well, maybe your babies would like these." He pulled his last pair of clean socks from the knapsack and handed them to the owl. "They can snuggle inside them at night, to keep warm."

Henrietta took the gift in her left talon and waved goodbye with the right. As she took off, she was laughing. "I don't think they can fit in your socks," she said as she left, "but they can wear them on their heads like caps. That will be a rare sight!"

As her joyful hoots faded gradually into the distance, Niles was left alone with Frederick, and with a distant hope that the ferret might leave the Endless Forest with him.

Chapter 25 - The Last Goodbye

Well, you knew it had to come sometime, and now is the time. Frederick too must leave so that Niles can truly finish his journey and return to his home.

On the grass by the path the two friends sat side by side, Frederick's head resting on Niles' leg, and Niles gently stroking the warm brown fur on the ferret's back.

"I have a question ... if you won't laugh too hard," Niles began. "When Henrietta was talking about her home and Claracuca's and Victorious', she never mentioned yours. Where is your home, Frederick? You said before that the Endless Forest was your home, but you must have someplace special, like with your mother and father."

"No, no, no," answered Frederick, "I don't live with my mother and father anymore. Not any more. We ferrets grow up and leave home younger than you do. It's been months since I went to find my own way. Mostly I just wander through the Forest. I like it here."

"Are you older than me?" asked Niles.

"In ferret years, I'm your age. Maybe a bit older. Just a bit." Frederick stopped for a moment and stared off into the trees. "But I would like a nice, warm comfortable home. Sometimes I would. Like when it gets cold in winter, and when there aren't many nuts to find. And when I get lonely."

That sat together for a time, not too long, not too short, not speaking. Niles gently smoothed the fur of Frederick's sleek coat. When he spoke again, Niles' voice was warm and supportive. Things had turned around, and now it was Niles who was trying to help the ferret to feel better. "What will you do now?" he asked.

"Now? Well, I'll explore the Forest some. There are berry bushes full of fruit by the Peppery Hills. Better than nuts. Well, sometimes better than some nuts. Then maybe I'll be part of someone else's journey. If I'm needed."

Niles was thoughtful. Something about the ferret seemed not to fit with the pattern of the Endless Forest. "You're not exactly like the other creatures of the forest, are you?" he asked suddenly.

Frederick was silent for quite a while, and Niles had begun to wonder if he shouldn't have asked that particular question. Finally, his friend responded. "No, I'm not. You are right. The others are all part of the Forest and also part of you. But that is all they are. There is nothing more to them. They are perfectly happy living their lives here."

It seemed to Niles that Fredcrick had said that last remark with a touch of bitterness. But he had no time to ponder that, as his friend continued: "But I _am_ different. I am part of the Forest, and I am part of you, but I am also partly just myself. I can never be fully content with other people's stories. I have one of my own, too."

Niles held his breath. Was it possible that his unvoiced dream could come true? Could Frederick leave the Endless Forest and live with him? Niles started to speak, hesitantly at first. "Can't you leave the Forest? Come live with me. I have a perfect home for you, and my mother and father won't mind. We can play together and I'll give you nuts every day, and ..."

Frederick smiled at him, but he also shook his head. "No," he interrupted, "it doesn't work that way. I can leave the Forest, and I do sometimes. I look for tasty nuts and berries. Sometimes for mice. But when I leave, I forget everything I knew in the Forest. I don't remember my forest life at all. Then, after a while, I get an urge and I come back here. As for you, you're not allowed to take me from the Endless Forest; it isn't permitted. You just can't do it."

"I can try," shouted Niles defiantly, and picking up the Frederick, he raised his voice and looked towards the sky. "My journey is finished. Take me home."

When nothing happened, he added: "Now!" Still nothing.

"Please." But it was clear that this just wasn't working. Niles put Frederick back on the ground, looked up at the sky showing between the tall forest trees, and shook his fist. "Okay," he shouted, "then I'll just stay here!"

As soon as he had said it, Niles knew it wasn't true. Frederick had been a very special forest friend, but his place was in the Endless Forest, and Niles' was not.

"Don't worry about me," said Frederick, "I really do like it here. And I couldn't live outside of the Endless Forest forever; remember, part of me is the Forest, just as part of me is you."

"I know," said Niles, softly and gently. "I must go, and very soon. But first, let me give you this present." He reached into his pocket and pulled out a marvelously smooth stone, his lucky stone, one which he had carried throughout the entire journey. Niles had used it when he needed strength and it had always helped. "It's my lucky stone," he said, "and maybe it will be lucky for you, too. I really don't have anything else to give you. I'm sorry."

For the one and only time in the entire journey, Frederick was speechless. He was so pleased with the gift that all he could do was to mumble something like "parting is such sweet sorrow." Even that wasn't original - somebody said it long ago, probably that William something-or-other guy.

"This is a very precious gift," Frederick finally was able to reply. "I will treasure it always. And now, goodbye my friend. You'll find my gift to you beneath that large oak tree." Grasping the lucky rock as tightly as he could and pointing awkwardly to a very large oak that overgrew the path, Frederick walked slowly off into the Endless Forest.

Niles tried not to think about missing Frederick and the rest of his forest friends. And, besides, he was getting very excited thinking about his home, his parents, Roger, and the rest of his other friends, not to mention all of the favorite things that he had had to leave behind when he went on this journey.

The Forest had given him that too, maybe the greatest gift of all. Because now Niles understood how much he valued what he had, and most especially his family and friends.

In fact, Niles was looking forward to going home so much that he nearly forgot about Frederick's gift. Nearly -- but not quite.

After all of the remarkable things that have happened in the Endless Forest, you may be disappointed to learn that Frederick's gift was only four nuts and three berries, wrapped carefully in an especially large oak leaf. But Niles wasn't disappointed in the slightest.

There was a walnut, a pecan, an acorn (which is really an oak nut), and an almond. The three berries were sodaberries, one purple, one red, and one yellow. They were all very large -- the walnut was the size of an egg! As Niles turned them over in his hand, he realized that each was perfect. The berries were firm and ripe, with no bruises or missing bits, and the nuts were evenly colored, solid and smooth.

Niles knew that Frederick must have been searching for just the right nuts and berries during the entire journey. All of those times, when Niles thought that the ferret was looking for something to eat or just playing around, he had actually been hunting for perfect gifts for Niles.

This would truly be the last thing Niles learned in the Endless Forest. He had a glimpse of how deep and rewarding friendship could be when it meant more than just playing together. At its best, friendship also meant doing things for the other person and then sharing in the joy that you have given.

This was just a vague idea inside of Niles' mind as he idly took one more step along the path. As he did, the shade of the Endless Forest gave way suddenly to bright sunshine. Niles held his hand over his eyes, shielding them from the unexpected light.

He was back. The forest was behind him, and the familiar path leading past Ms. Greenstem's garden to his own home lay ahead.

Chapter 26 - Who Will Ever Believe It?

Niles looked wistfully back at the Endless Forest, now just a fringe of trees at the end of a sunny meadow. He paused, wondering if he would ever see his forest friends again. But then the thought of home, of parents, of his own room and his own bed -- all of these drew him as irresistibly as he had been drawn into the Forest four days before.

Fighting back an impulse to run, Niles set out, walking briskly. Soon the hills between the forest and his home lay behind him and his path widened. One more curve and the larger path from the village and his school appeared on his right, gradually approaching and merging with the forest path.

Niles slowed his pace. A thought had just occurred to him. "What will I tell Mom and Dad? They'll never believe the truth. They'll flip if I tell them I was even in the Endless Forest."

Niles half expected some nasty remarks from Calamidrake, but none came. At least that situation was under control.

He had very little time to ponder his problem before Ms. Greenstem's house came into view and his own home just beyond. Niles walked more quickly, almost running

now, but as he approached Ms. Greenstem's, a thought popped into his mind.

To Niles it seemed like the right thing to do, perhaps the only thing to do, and so he went ahead and did it without thinking any more about whether he should or not. Sometimes you have to trust your feelings.

Apparently, Ms. Greenstem wasn't home; at least, her windows were closed and all the blinds were drawn. Her garden was as beautiful as ever, filled with flowers of dazzling color and delicate shape -- petunias, chrysanthemums, fragrant purple, pink and white stock, and many others whose names Niles could not even guess.

However, one corner of the garden, the one furthest from the house, was bare. Before his journey, Niles, urged on by Calamidrake, had spray-painted the plants in this section with a can of black paint. Ms. Greenstem must have removed these and hadn't gotten around to planting anything else yet.

Niles knelt on the rich green grass next to the empty garden corner. Using a stick he found on the ground, he dug several small holes in the garden soil. Reaching into his back pants pocket, he pulled out his handkerchief and carefully unfolded it. There, Niles found the seeds that Morning Gloria had given him. He placed a few in each hole.

Next, he brought out the walnut shell wrapped with honeysuckle vine and filled with the dirt from the Endless Forest. Niles placed a small amount of this magical soil into each hole and gently patted it down. Last, Niles reached into his backpack for the jelly jar full of Itasara's water. It was perfectly clear and seemed to sparkle in the rays of the Sun. He wet the soil with a bit of the precious water and then screwed the top firmly back on the jar.

Niles knew that he needed to do something to make up for the damage he had done to Ms. Greenstem's garden. Besides, he kind of liked her; she always gave cookies to the kids who played near her house. Even Niles had gotten some a few times.

Niles also made sure he had some seeds, some soil, and some water left for himself. These he would use in the coming weeks to grow a morning glory plant in a pot in his room, a pot that looked very much like the one in which Morning Gloria had grown.

Now Niles could delay no longer. No matter what his parents would say to him, the time to return to his own home had come. The Sun was already setting in the West, its color changing to a deep yellow with a hint of orange. Dusting off his hands, Niles packed the walnut shell and the jelly jar into his backpack, and began to walk the last hundred steps to his home.

Reaching the door, Niles unlocked it and stepped into his own living room. His parents weren't home. That was a relief. Niles wanted a few minutes to enjoy this most wonderful of houses before having to explain things to his mother and father. Although the sofa looked comfortable and tempting, it was his own room that drew Niles. Bounding up the stairs two at a time, he flung open his

bedroom door, half expecting that it would somehow be very different from the way he had left it. After all, _he_ was very different from what he had been four days ago.

But the room was exactly the way it had been before his journey. For some reason that brought a great feeling of comfort to Niles. Even when you experience great change, many things stay the same. Niles was glad that this was so. He was beginning to understand that although parts of his life had been very disturbing (especially those parts that involved Calamidrake), still much of it was good and some of it quite excellent. His room, for example. These things had not been lost during his great journey.

The thought made him smile, then laugh, and then kick off his shoes and jump onto his bed. I'm afraid Niles' clothes were very dirty. He probably should have taken a bath and changed into clean things before rolling around in his bed. But Niles wasn't thinking about that now -- it was just so good to be home!

The Endless Forest had allowed him to learn how to control the Dragon, and many other things. Now he had these learnings and strengths plus all of the wonderful things that had been his before the journey - his room, his racing cars, his home, his parents, his friends. Only one small cloud marred the perfect moment. Niles could not help thinking about Frederick, and wishing that the pesky little ferret could be here to share everything with him.

Actually, Niles was forgetting something. But just then, the sound of a car pulling up into the gravel driveway reminded him. His parents. They had come home and, in a few moments, he would have to decide exactly how to explain to them where he had been during the last four days. But then he remembered Henrietta saying that time was different in the Endless Forest; Niles hoped that was true. He decided that if his parents didn't say anything about him being away for four days, he wouldn't either.

Niles really should not have worried - Henrietta had clearly told him that only a small part of a day would have passed when he got out of the Endless Forest. But Niles wasn't thinking that clearly now.

In any case, the door opened and Niles could not restrain himself. He had missed his mother and father much more than he wished to admit, and so his legs took over, as they often did, and carried him down the stairs even faster than he had run up them minutes before.

His mother had just stepped into the house when Niles was upon her, grabbing her around the waist and hugging her. Of course, she didn't know that Niles had been away, so this display of affection surprised her. But one thing about Niles' mother -- and about all mothers that I have ever known -- they never question it when their children show their love.

She just hugged Niles back, and gave him a little kiss on the top of the head. This was not one of Niles' favorite gestures but he endured it. "She won't be able to do that much longer," thought Niles, squirming a little. "Pretty soon I'll be taller than she is."

Closing the door behind him, Niles' father voiced the question that had been worrying Niles. "So, what have you been up to?" he asked, brushing himself off a little. Niles was pretty dusty and some of it had ended up on his parent's clothes. They weren't angry about it, and in fact hardly even noticed. That's one of the advantages of being Niles' age -- you can be dirty, up to a point, and no one complains about it.

Niles had decided to tell the truth, even if no one believed him. But the situation didn't seem to demand a detailed answer, so he put off the long explanation and answered simply. "Just messing around," he said. That was at least partly true -- he was certainly a mess.

In any case, that seemed to satisfy his dad. Mom looked at him skeptically, but since she didn't ask any more questions, Niles didn't feel he had to give any more answers. Besides, at that very moment, both the phone and the doorbell rang and a familiar voice called out "Anybody home?" It was Roger!

His parents went to answer the phone, but Niles bolted to the door, grabbed the knob, and practically threw the door open. "Roger," he cried out in delight, "come in. Come on in!"

Roger stepped through the doorway, looking at Niles quizzically. What had made his friend so incredibly happy? He soon had it figured out. "You've been there," he stated.

"Yes," said Niles. "And now I'm back."

There was no need for Roger to ask if the journey had been a success; it was obvious from Niles' face and joyous energy. Roger put his arm around Niles' shoulders and they both plunked down on the sofa.

Niles realized that here was the perfect person to listen to his story, and he was about to begin it when his father came into the room. He glanced at the sofa and then at Niles' still dusty shirt and pants. "Maybe you can find some cleaner clothes," he suggested.

Niles was horrified. Had he gotten that old? Was his allowance to be dirty, up to a point, a thing of the past? He knew it would happen as he grew up -- that was part of the price for becoming a young man -- but Niles wished it hadn't happened at precisely this moment. Before he could get up, however, his Dad went on.

"Never mind, you can do it later." ("That's a relief," thought Niles). "I have something else to talk to you about." He sat down on the big chair that faced the sofa.

Roger got up to leave, but Niles' father stopped him. "You can stay, Roger. This isn't any secret."

"The strangest thing just happened to your mother and I. We were driving back from the market and passed by the edge of the Deep Woods. Suddenly, I saw something in the middle of the road -- some kind of animal. I had to brake very hard to avoid hitting it because it didn't move, even when I blew the horn. I got out to see if the poor thing was hurt, but it didn't seem to be. Then I recognized what it was -- it was a ferret! Can you believe it? A ferret sitting right out in the middle of the road!"

To say that Niles was surprised would be to say too little. He was astounded. This was good luck beyond anything he could have dreamed. A ferret of his own -- Niles was sure his father would let him keep it. Briefly a fantastic notion flickered in his heart. Maybe this ferret was Frederick! But Niles knew that couldn't be. It was enough that he was going to have a ferret. It couldn't replace Frederick in his heart, but what a wonderful reminder and friend it would be. "Where is it, Dad?" he blurted out.

His father laughed. He had hoped Niles would want to keep the ferret as a pet. Niles' father knew that Niles had been troubled and that there had been many problems in the boy's life. He and Niles' mother had talked about getting Niles a dog or maybe a cat. (Niles would probably have been okay with the dog, but the cat was a terrible idea -- Niles considered cats to be nuisances at best.)

Niles' father went into the kitchen and returned promptly, holding a beautiful ferret, with sleek brown and tan fur, and black and white markings. His father handed the animal to Niles. It nestled in his arms contentedly. Niles smiled. His Dad smiled. His Mom smiled. Roger wanted to hold the ferret.

Niles knew that he would take the very best of care of his newest friend. The ferret seemed to know it too, because although he would allow all of the family members to pick him up and stroke his soft fur, he was most comfortable with Niles, and that is where he went whenever he had the chance.

The next day, Niles' parents went to town and bought a cage for the new family member. I am sorry to say, however, that the cage got almost no use at all. Niles would not allow it to be locked, so the ferret used it only as a place to find water and food. Most of the rest of the time it spent in Niles' room, which was full of the wonderful nooks and corners that ferrets love.

His Mom and Dad, Roger, and just about everyone at school had been asking him what the ferret's name was, but Niles had been reluctant to give it a name. He wanted to name it after his forest friend, but there was still some sadness in his heart when these memories came upon him, so Niles had just left his pet unnamed.

About a week later, however, he decided the time had to come. Gradually, the pain of leaving his friends had diminished. It was a turning point for Niles. He was ending once and for all that part of his life that had led up to his journey, and beginning the next part.

Sitting on his bed, Niles carefully picked up his new pet. "It's time I gave you a name," he said softly, "and I've decided to call you Freddie. It's a very dear name to me, but you've become special too, and I want you to have it."

The ferret seemed unimpressed. After all, what could Niles expect. Only in the Endless Forest was he able to talk with animals. It was too much to expect his newest friend to understand what a name was. In fact, the ferret looked positively annoyed.

There was a knock on his bedroom door, and Niles' father came in the room to say "good night." They talked for a little while. Just as he was leaving, his father noticed Freddie on Niles' bed. "Shouldn't he sleep in his cage?" he asked dubiously. But seeing that Niles began to get upset by the suggestion, he quickly dropped it.

"Okay, okay, let him sleep here! It doesn't look like I have much choice. You're just as stubborn as that animal. Do you know, when we found it, it was clutching a rock in its paws. Even when I picked it up, it would not let go of that rock. Finally, when we got home, I pried it loose and put in the trash can. And would you believe it, the ferret jumped out of my arms and pawed through the trash until it got that rock back! I think he dragged it into his cage and hid it under that old blanket you gave him. Stubborn. Well, good night ... to both of you." He closed the bedroom door behind him as he left.

Niles' was puzzled. "A rock," he thought, "what would a ferret want with a rock?"

You can imagine, I expect, Niles' surprise (which quickly turned into astonishment) when, squirming out of his grasp, and standing up as tall as it could on its hind feet, the ferret answered him.

"It was your lucky rock, dummy! ... And I told you -- my name is Frederick!"

About the Authors

Miriam M. Gottlieb, Ph.D. is the author of *The Angry Self: A Comprehensive Approach to Anger Management* published in 1999 by Zeig, Tucker, & Theisen, Incorporated. She is a licensed psychologist in Scottsdale, Arizona and has been practicing for 40 years. Dr. Gottlieb has had the privilege of working with diverse populations and age ranges in multiple settings. The inspiration for *The Endless Forest* was borne after a session with a 10-year-old boy who had difficulty understanding why he got in trouble so often. This boy liked stories, so, before he moved out of state, Dr. Gottlieb gifted him with a short story which became the foundation for this book. Dr. Gottlieb enjoys telling stories and does so through writing and photography.

David M. Gottlieb, Ph.D. was the author of the Wally the Walrus series (not yet published) which he wrote for his granddaughter Ika. Dr. Gottlieb obtained a Ph.D. in astrophysics from the University of Maryland. His love of the universe began when he was five years old, at the time when he decided he would become an astronomer. Dr. Gottlieb worked briefly as an astronomer for NASA, and then changed careers to developing computer software, where he authored many technical documents. Dr. Gottlieb's writing skills easily transferred from technical documents to children's fiction. Dr. Gottlieb's wit and clever dialogue entertain the reader throughout *The Endless Forest*. Dr. Gottlieb passed away on April 15, 2020 of Covid19.

Acknowledgements

I would like to thank David (of blessed memory) my beloved husband, who graciously collaborated and coauthored this book. This story might have remained just a story without his significant contributions. David made the characters in The Endless Forest come alive with his witty dialogue; more than his clever contributions was his unwavering support not only in the writing of this story, but in all aspects of our life together.

Thank you, Daniel, my son, for never underestimating your mother, for your enthusiasm and support of the publication of this book, and for being the "Frederick" during my recent journey through the endless forest. Thank you, Lauren, for loving my son.

Also grateful to Ika, my favorite granddaughter, for being a source of constant inspiration and filling my heart with overflowing love.

Thank you, Sara, Victor (of blessed memory), Gloria, Henry, and Clara, my siblings, who inspired the characters in this story and who shared the special "growing-up journey" that only siblings can share. I am grateful to their spouses and their children, my nieces and nephews, and their children, for being an important part of my life.

I am particularly grateful to Benjamin Fine Katz, my great nephew (and he is truly a great guy), Clara's grandson, who spent endless hours on zoom guiding his great aunt through this process with incredible kindness.

I am grateful to the "Rogers" in my life, my dearest and closest friends (you know who you are) for being part of life's journey.

Thank you to my oldest friend (friends for 67 years), Julie Colantonio Marelli (formerly Julie Kris) for being a friend for life and for being so very present during sad and happy times; Eva Efune, my 90-year-old friend, who has encouraged my writing through the years and whose fortitude is a source of inspiration; and Nellie Cronin, my neighbor and newest friend, who understands the importance of "walking the walk" and living a life with purpose. I am indebted to all for their gifts and for making this a better world.

Yes, I could go on and on and on, for there is much for which to be thankful and many to whom I am grateful, but I will end with one giant heartfelt thank you to all the people in my life who permanently reside in my heart and who inspire me to be better.

Made in the USA
Middletown, DE
16 November 2021

52469113R00129